He Loves Me, He Loves You Not 3

In Love Lies Misery

A novel

MYCHEA

Good2Go Publishing

Published by:
GOOD2GO PUBLISHING
7311 W. Glass Lane
Laveen, AZ 85339
www.good2gopublishing.com
Twitter @good2gobooks
G2G@good2gopublishing.com
Facebook.com/good2gopublishing
ThirdLane Marketing: Brian James
Brian@good2gopublishing.com

Cover Design: Davida Baldwin
Editor: Me'Shell Stewart
ISBN: 978-0996060950

Books by This Author

Coveted

Vengeance

He Loves Me, He Loves You Not

He Loves Me, He Loves You Not 2 Puppetmaster

He Loves Me, He Loves You Not 3

My Boyfriend's Wife

Acknowledgments

To my amazing readers, I appreciate you always!

Hugs and Kisses

~M~

PRELUDE

Time was of the essence. Phylicia felt as if the entire world was after her. She had to move quickly and take everything in stride. The police suspected that she would be going after Trent and his family, but she had other arrangements in mind. Blond wig, tanned skin and sunglasses; she resembled Storm from X-Men. This disguise afforded her the opportunity to hide in plain sight. Her target was in view and she meant to take it out…by any means necessary.

****

Natalia felt uneasy. She'd been in Miami Beach for months hiding from her old life while trying to blend into her new one.

Today was her first day outside on the beach. She hadn't been able to take being cooped up in the boarding house for another second. She stayed inside for her own protection, attempting to give Phylicia time to cool down. She knew Phylicia was out there somewhere looking for her, which is why she had gone to great lengths to disappear. Even though the beach was full of people, she thought to herself, "How much danger could I really be in?" as she laid her blanket on the sand to get some sun.

"Hi." Natalia glanced up, as a very handsome man looked down, smiling at her. Natalia flipped over and smiled uneasily. She had just laid out on the beach and this man popped up out of thin air.

"Hello." She replied, sitting up on her blanket.

"Mind if I join you?" He asked, plopping down before Natalia had a chance to decline his offer.

"I'd rather be alone, if you don't mind." Natalia told him, not wanting to offend. She nervously kept checking her surroundings. Unable to trusting anyone, she felt exposed.

Standing abruptly, she gathered up her blanket. Without looking back at him, she made her way back to her room.

Back in her room at the house, Natalia began to relax. She hated feeling troubled. She wasn't the scared type, but not being familiar with the territory was putting her at an extreme disadvantage.

Opening her closet door, Natalia reached for her bathrobe. She cocked her head to the side, frowning when she realized that it wasn't there. She could have sworn she had left it hanging on the door hanger.

"Looking for this?" Natalia froze when she heard the familiar voice on the other side of her closet door. Cursing herself because she'd left her switchblade in the bag; she carried to the beach, which was now next to the door.

Pulling the closet door closed, Natalia faced her nemesis Phylicia. Natalia took in the blond wig, oversized sunglasses, and darkly tanned skin.

"You thought you could get away from me? I own you or did you forget?" Phylicia asked in a menacing tone. "Now sit down," she ordered Natalia.

Natalia was many things, but a punk she was not. If Phylicia wanted her to do anything, she was going to have to make her, plain and simple.

"No," she told her in a firm, confident tone.

"No?" Phylicia repeated. She then removed a small hatchet from her bag and bashed Natalia's kneecap in.

Natalia immediately dropped to the ground screaming in agony. Phylicia's face lit up like a kid in a candy store as she watched Natalia squirming around on the floor, clutching her knee.

Phylicia kneeled on the floor in front of her, "See what you made me do?" She began shaking her head, "If you had only done as I asked, you wouldn't be in this situation now. How does your knee feel?" She asked Natalia sweetly.

Natalia was in blinding pain, she knew her kneecap was shattered.

Phylicia stood and watched Natalia withering around on the ground like a snake.

"You know the really crazy part about this situation, Natalia? Phylicia spoke while removing a knife from her bag. I respect you." If only things had been different. If only you hadn't set me up to take a fall so that you could have Trent... you and I would have made an amazing team. I admire your spirit and tenacity." Phylicia looked down at her, "In another life, the two of us would have been friends."

Natalia snorted. "Not in any lifetime could we have been friends."

Phylicia's eyes flashed angrily when she heard Natalia's comment. Sinking to her knees on the floor, Phylicia grabbed Natalia's face and held it in her hands, remembering her as the little girl she had met all those years ago.

"I know. I know what your brother did to you. I know all the years that he molested you and you felt like you had no one to turn to. I understand being angry with me for not stepping in to help. You thought as his wife, I should have saved you, right?"

Phylicia felt the hot moisture flowing from her eyes. "And maybe I would have been able to if I had been able to save myself. But I couldn't save either of us. He helped to make me this way."

"You did nothing to help me. Then you took Trent from me."

Phylicia let her face go and stared at her as if she were delusional. "I didn't know you were dating Trent. You were holding onto a grudge for no good reason. I didn't know about you. Trent came after me. You should have put on your big girl panties and let it go like any mature woman would have."

"You were married to my brother!" Natalia spat at her. "I thought you would have had the decency to respect your marriage."

"You know what kind of monster Maxwell was. There was no love lost there."

"You're both monsters!"

"Yeah?" Phylicia stared at her, "And what about you? Stop trying to be the innocent here. You're not."

"I am the innocent. Maxwell raped me for *all* my teenage years. You don't get over things like that, you just don't."

"You're preaching to the choir, Natalia. You're my sister-in-law and I love you, but I can't forgive you for what you did to me. That is the ultimate betrayal and I'm done discussing this with you." Raising her hand quickly, Phylicia jabbed the knife's blade into the center of Natalia's throat and cut all the way down to her collarbone. Blood splattered on Phylicia's face as she made the cut. Pushing the blade further in, she retraced the gash she'd made. After removing the knife from Natalia's flesh, Phylicia wiped it off on the blanket that Natalia had with her on the beach. She then wiped her face, grabbed her bag and left the room just as silently as she had come.

****

Phylicia slowly approached the happy family who were oblivious to her presence. A flurry of commotion made her halt in her tracks. Police officers were running toward her from every direction. Breath catching in her throat, Phylicia let the weapon in her hand go and quickly looked down busying herself inside the bag she carried.

She sighed a breath of relief as the officers pushed past her to enter the hotel that she had recently vacated. Phylicia glanced at the family that she had been pursuing. She felt a rush of energy take over her when she made eye contact with Trent, who had glanced in her direction from the commotion of the police, and recognizing her immediately.

Offering up a quirky smile and silent salute, Phylicia made a hasty retreat, attempting to put as much distance between her and the police as she could. Trent and his family would live to see another day. She thoroughly hoped that they enjoyed the little amount of time that she was going to allow them. She would continue her pursuit of them in the near future and their day would definitely come. Much sooner than later she thought.

He Loves Me,
He Loves You Not 3
In Love Lies Misery

He will never be rid of me,

,but there comes a time when the games must end and I must

tell him goodbye,

May his soul rest in peace,

,or as much peace that I have allowed him to have,

CHAPTER 1

"Happy Birthday to you, happy birthday to you, happy birthday to you, happy birthday to Avionne, happy birthday to you! And many more!" Avionne's friends sang out to her in merriment. Her foster mother Krista stood back from the crowd and smiled with tears in her eyes, finding it hard to believe that the thirteen-year-old girl she had taken in seven years ago and was twenty years old today. She was so proud of her. Avionne had been a model child. Knowledgeable, well beyond her years, she graduated high school at the age of fifteen and college at the age of nineteen, both with honors. She would now be leaving for law school within the next month.

Watching her with all of her friends, it felt as if just yesterday the social worker dropped her off at the house.

Looking at her now, she was a beautiful, young woman all grown up. Her baby. Krista thought, smiling. As Avionne ran up to her, she held out the keys to her brand new black Toyota Corolla.

"Thanks Mom. You are the greatest," Avionne said removing the keys from her hand and giving her a kiss on the cheek.

Krista laughed as she tapped her grown-up baby's nose. "No, sweetie, you are a momma's dream and I love you," Avionne smiled at her, "Now get outta here and have fun." She blinked rapidly trying not to let the tears fall.

"Yes, ma'am. I'd be a fool to turn down that offer. See you later."

Krista smiled as the party began to wrap up and the kids began making their exit to go to other parties.

****

On a hilltop not too far away hidden by a line of trees, Phylicia sent up a silent happy birthday to her daughter from where she sat watching her party. She smiled at how adult-like she had become. Avionne wasn't a little girl anymore; she was a grown woman now. Phylicia regretted that she had missed all the years of her growing up. The two of them would never be able to get back these were moments in time. She knew it was only a matter of time before the tears misted in her eyes and clouded her vision. She hated to admit, even to herself, that other than Trent, Avionne was the biggest weakness for her.

Phylicia allowed herself to be tortured only twice a year by checking on her daughter. That's all the time that she could allot for maternal emotions and the added risk of being caught. Observing as the crowd shifted, her breath caught when she saw her. Her baby girl was in plain view getting something from her foster mother and smiling as she kissed her. That's when the tears fell. Phylicia could handle many things, but this would be tough for anybody. She wanted to go over to them so badly. She wanted to give her baby a hug and tell her how much she loved her, but the time wasn't right yet. Rising slowly to her feet, she walked closer to the house. She was getting too emotional and she knew it. She wanted to see if she could get into the house that her daughter lived in and remove recent photos of her. Keeping to the edge of the trees, Phylicia watched as her daughter drove by her with friends in her car laughing and joking around. She smiled again at how pretty and happy she looked. Avionne would never guess in a million years that she had just driven by her *missing and wanted* mother.

After seeing what she needed to see in the house and copping a few of the framed photos of Avionne as a teenager and now, Phylicia began the thirty-minute hike back to her car to begin her journey back to her home. She had to be careful these days; she knew she would have to relocate again soon. America's Most Wanted had played a segment on her again last night.

This was the third time in ten years she'd seen it aired. Whenever it was shown was when the most heat came down on her the hardest. She had to continue the run so they could continue the hunt.

****

Upon entering the house and shutting the door…without cutting on any of the lights, Avionne could sense that something was wrong. She couldn't put a finger on it, but the tingling feeling down her spine was becoming more prominent. Reaching over to cut the light switch on, Avionne was slightly annoyed when no light illuminated the room. Figuring the bulbs had blown; she pulled her new mini flashlight out her bag and looked around. Everything appeared normal, but it wasn't. Where was her foster mother, Krista? Making her way to the kitchen, she flicked that switch too and nothing happened. Almost instantaneously, a wave of dread washed over her. Pulling her hand away from the switch, she realized that it was wet and sticky. Guiding the flashlight to look at her hands, Avionne's heart sank. Her hand was covered in blood.

Avionne's head and heart began to pound simultaneously. All of a sudden, she was having a hard time breathing. The air in her lungs was quickly running out. She felt as if she were suffocating in her own skin.

Hearing the front door slam, Avionne quickly turned off the flashlight and pressed herself flat against the wall. She didn't want to be found in the kitchen like this in the event that someone may think something suspicious was going on.

"Avi, you in here?"

Avionne sighed a breath of relief when she heard her foster sister Kamilah's voice yelling out to her.

"Yeah, I'm here." Avionne yelled back, while exiting the kitchen more at ease with herself.

"Something is up with our electricity. I called the electric company and they should be fixing the problem soon."

"Good," Avionne said, as she walked up to Kamilah to give her a hug. "I was worried; I thought something had happened to you."

Kamilah let out a laugh, "Why? Because the lights are off? Avi, you have got to lighten up. You've been so uptight lately. You okay?"

"I know," Avon said, releasing Kamilah. "I have got to learn how to relax. I don't know what is going on with me."

"Hey, have you seen Tiki?" Kamilah asked, abruptly switching topics, "I've been calling out to her, but she won't stop hiding."

The ever-present dread feeling returned. Now Avionne knew what the blood in the kitchen was from. Tiki was Kamilah's Senegalese cat. She had gotten Tiki when she was twelve years old as a gift from her biological father, who had passed away.

"Uh Kami, maybe you should sit down," Avionne began slowly.

"What's wrong?" Kamilah enveloped Avionne in a hug. "What is going on? It's your birthday you can't be so down like this."

Avionne opened her mouth to speak, but before a word could come out the lights flickered back on.

"Lights!" Kamilah exclaimed as she released Avionne and turned to survey the room. "Great. Tiki! Where are you?" Kamilah turned back to face Avionne, "It's not like her to be this quiet. You think she's hiding or something. Maybe she's in the kitchen eating?" She said as she headed for the kitchen doorway.

Avionne stayed where she was not anxious to see what gruesome scene was probably waiting in the kitchen.

Everyone in the neighborhood could hear Kamilah's blood curling scream, Avionne was sure of it. Staying rooted to the spot that she was in, she watched as Kamilah came running out the kitchen with a haunted look on her face and a very alive and intact Tiki in her arms- visibly shaken.

"It's, it's a... a," Kamilah was stuttering so badly that Avionne had no choice, but to go look in the kitchen to see what was going on. Walking apprehensively into the kitchen, she stopped short. There, hanging from their ceiling, was their foster mother Krista. Avionne could see that her neck was broken as it hung from the rope. Feeling her heart leap into her throat, Avionne stared at the body hanging from the ceiling for what seemed like an eternity. Krista had been her mother for the past seven years. The best mother anyone could ever ask for and now she was gone, which meant Avionne had no one now.

Leaving the kitchen, she walked past Kamilah without saying a word and went to her room. Throwing some of her clothes and other belongings in a bag, she hated knowing that her foster mother's body was hanging in the kitchen, but she knew that she couldn't stay around this chaos. She needed to put as much distance between herself and this place as humanly possible. Walking back into the living room, she saw Kamilah hunched on the sofa with Tiki in her arms. Without so much as a goodbye, Avionne crept out the door. It's not that she didn't love Krista and Kamilah, because she did. Yet, no one knew the true story about her background and who her biological mother was. If she stayed in that house, with that body hanging like that, someone was sure to do their research and try to place the blame on her and she couldn't have that.

She couldn't have that at all.

CHAPTER 2

Several hours later, Phylicia pulled into the parking garage of her rented home. The house she rented was nice, but she had rented this one for a particular reason. Cutting off the lights in the car, she patiently sat and watched for the person she was waiting for to arrive. This was her daily routine… to watch for this particular individual's arrival. Hearing footsteps behind her, Phylicia put on her sunglasses and watched as the woman walked by her car and up the steps to her own house. Phylicia's hatred for this woman was so great. The two of them had been neighbors for about two weeks now. She hated all this moving, but the program the woman was in required her and her family to move every few years.

Getting out of the car a short time after the woman had gone in, Phylicia followed the route the woman had taken only moments earlier and bid her time.

****

"Remi, did you wash the dishes in the sink?" Shia yelled toward the kitchen as she walked into the house from her favorite place the HomeGoods store.

Rolling her eyes, Remi sighed and began running water into the deep stainless steel sink. Even though she was a grown woman, she never felt that way around her twin sisters. They always treated her like a child. At twenty-eight years old, she was a woman and she needed them to accept and respect what she thought, as she put her hands into the soapy water and began washing the dishes, feeling like a modern day Cinderella.

"Let me help you with that. I've told you about standing on chairs and reaching up to fix the curtains." Trent said a short while later when he walked into the living room only to find his wife standing in one of the dining room chairs in which she'd dragged into the room attempting to put the curtains up.

"Yes Sir." Shia replied, smirking while lowering herself down from the chair as Trent lightly scolded her. He had the tendency of treating her with kid gloves, as if she was fragile. "I'm pretty sure that I can handle standing in a chair without falling out of it, boo."

"I'm sure you can," Trent said as he fixed the curtain for her, "but I'd rather not risk it." He looked down at her, "If that's okay with you."

"Guess it's going to have to be." Shia laughed as she gazed up into his eyes. "I love you."

The two of them had been through a lot over the years. Even after all this time and all of their trials, they were still a team unit… in it to win it.

"I love you more. You know I'm sorry about all of this, right?" Trent asked her.

"It's not your fault babe," she told him. This was their fifth move in two years. With this move, they had been relocated to

Charlotte, NC. They were both northern city people and Shia wondered how this southern city living would work out for them. Making her way to their master bedroom, she began filing papers on her desk that she'd taken out of a box titled "loose papers" earlier that morning. Unfolding a letter, she was surprised to have happened across a poem that Trent had written her in their first year of marriage.

The beauty of things to come
as time goes by
the smiles of yesterday
long afternoons in hidden spaces
touches that set your heart on fire
the comfort of silence
whispered words during heated moments
tingly feelings down your spine
fingers that go on everlasting journeys
teeth that gently graze your earlobe
sighs in the dark
the joy of a babies laughter
grievances of a funeral march
rainbows after the storm
sunny afternoons;

MYCHEA

a cool breeze

unsuspected surprises

at unusual moments

promises of memories in time

passion under starry night skies

mornings that come too soon

eyes filled with promise

from kindled moments

time ticking by slowly, slowly

yet going by so quickly

the laughter

the tears

expressions of love

for my wife Shia

I will always love you

Trent

Shia pressed the poem up to her chest directly above her
heart, knowing there was no way she could love Trent any more
than she already did. Placing the poem in the file with the rest of
her papers, she moved on to finish the final box of clothing she
had. Pulling the last of her sweaters out of the final box that the
movers left in her closet, she placed it on a hanger and hung it

up. She didn't want to complain because she was happy to still be alive, but she was tired of moving. She was ready to snatch her hair out by its roots if she had to relocate one more time.

Sighing in frustration, she hung the sweaters in the closet. She then walked over to the large window in her and Trent's bedroom that faced towards the street. Staring out at her rural surroundings, a lone tear slid down her face and she began to wonder how much longer she could live her life on the run like this. More than anything, she wanted her children to be able to put down roots somewhere. Shia felt as if there was a disconnect between her life and the real world.

"I know." Trent whispered as he came up behind her and wrapped his arms around her waist, "I'm tired of moving as well." He whispered in her ear. Knowing what was wrong without having to ask. After a certain amount of years of marriage, he knew his wife like the back of his hand.

Shia's eyes met his in the reflection of the bay-style window as she allowed her body to relax in her husband's embrace. Trent dipped his head down to kiss the top of Shia's head.

"I want this to be over. We cannot run from Phylicia forever." Shia paused before continuing. "Our children deserve to be able to live a normal life."

Trent felt her body trembling in anger. Removing his hands from her waist, he turned her toward the bed so that they could continue their conversation there. Shia allowed him to guide her onto their king-sized Tempur-Pedic bed.

"Shy, I know these past few years of constantly moving so abruptly have been rough on all of us, but I know, especially for you." Reaching up, he ran his thumb down her cheek erasing evidence of the tear that had trailed there.

"What can I do to make you happy?" Trent asked. He knew that his wife was suffering internally. Every time their family was uprooted, a piece of her once bright personality died. He had an eerie feeling that she was distancing herself from him and he was somehow losing her.

"Stay and fight." Shia spoke lowly, "We can't run away from her anymore." Shia shook her head as her eyes began to mist. "We just can't."

Trent sat on the floor in front of the bed facing Shia, their eyes doing an emotional tango as they gazed at one another.

"Ok." Trent told her. "We won't run anymore."

"Do you think that's selfish?" Shia asked him softly, even though she was glad he had given in so readily, "I don't want our children in danger by any means, but they cannot grow up like this." Shia lowered her head, "They just can't."

"I agree." Trent said, grabbing her hand. "We'll figure it out. Okay?" He said bringing her hand to his lips. "Okay." Shia replied.

****

Phylicia almost laughed as she watched Trent and his family settle into their new place. She thought it was pure comedy that they thought they could get away from her. She was always one-step ahead of them. FBI protection was only good if the FBI actually protected and didn't tell anyone where the protected family was going to be.

As their children play outside in the yard, Phylicia envisioned what it would be like to be with Trent again raising their little family together. Because of him, she was running out of time to have more babies. Avionne, her first-born baby girl was twenty years old. Phylicia could hardly believe it herself sometimes. She was so proud of her baby. Even without being present in her life, Avionne was following in her footsteps by being in a pre-law program studying to be an attorney. Phylicia couldn't be prouder that her seed would amount to be a better woman than her mother was. That's all that she could hope for was that she would have a better life.

Phylicia had to admit in her own life, she was tiring of chasing Trent all over the country. Maybe it is time to leave this crazy world behind, she thought. I'm tired of this. Focusing her attention back on Trent's yard, she noticed that the smallest child looking to be about three was all by herself giggling, running around, and chasing butterflies. Completing a quick surveillance of the yard and the windows, Phylicia saw no one looking. Moving swiftly like a thief in the night, she picked up the little girl, while covering her mouth with her hand and sprinted to her car. It was time to start a new life and what better way than as a mom finally having the opportunity to raise a daughter all her own.

****

Hearing the lively chatter from the kitchen, indicating her children were back in doors. Shia made her way down the curved stairway.

"Hey you guys."

"Hi, mom." Five jolly voices without a care in the world echoed back at her.

"Where's Luna?" Shia asked, not seeing her youngest daughter. "She was outside with you all, right?"

"Oh yeah!" Joelle, Shia, and Trent's thirteen-year-old spoke, "Can't believe we forgot her, I'll get her," she said running back out the house shouting Luna's name.

Shia narrowed her eyes, glaring at her sixteen-year-old twin boys, Kyle and Ryder, who was joking and laughing at the kitchen table, eating chocolate chip cookies oblivious to their mother's rage.

"I cannot believe you two left your three year old sister outside alone." She scolded them, "You're supposed to look out for your little sisters. That's what responsible older brothers do."

"Sorry mom." Their deep voices spoke in unison as they lowered their heads ashamed of themselves.

"I don't see her." A panicked Joelle stated as she burst through the door.

Shia's heart slammed into her chest.

"What do you mean you don't see her?" She screamed running toward the backyard.

"TRENT," she yelled. "TRENT," she continued yelling as she ran out the backdoor.

"Luna…Luna." Shia yelled repeatedly as she ran around the house to the front yard and out into the street seeing no signs of her baby girl.

"LUNA!" Shia screamed from the middle of the street. Curious neighbors began coming out their houses.

"You okay Miss?"

"No, I'm not okay." Shia snapped in between breaths, her chest heaving up and down from all of the running she had been doing. "My daughter is missing."

Shia sunk to her knees in the street crying uncontrollably. Trent made his way to her side.

"Baby, what is going on?" He asked kneeling down in front of her as cars beeped at them because they were forced to go around the duo that seemed to be oblivious that they were obstructing traffic.

"Luna is missing. The kids left her outside alone." Shia sobbed, "I knew it was only a matter of time before she got a hold of us."

Trent looked at Shia strange. "Before who got hold of us? Have you checked the house just in case? You know how Luna enjoys a good game of hide and seek." Trent spoke slow and calm. It's not that he wasn't concerned for his daughter as well, but someone needed to remain calm and Shia was borderline hysterical at the moment.

"You know who!" She snapped. Shia looked at his face flushed red and covered in tears before softening her tone a little. "You think she can be playing a game of hide and seek?"

Trent tilted his head, "Maybe, you never know. Let's get you out of the street and check the house just in case." Standing up, he placed his hands under her arms and slowly guided Shia to her feet and began walking her towards the house.

The children all stood in the backyard watching their parents with solemn expressions on their faces.

"We checked the house, she's not here." Kyle told his parents as soon as they were within hearing distance.

Shia brushed past her children in a zombie like state. She needed to check every crevice of the house for herself. She wasn't relying on the word of her children, not one of them.

Trent painfully watched as Shia searched every nook and cranny of the house. He had Ryder call the police and he could hear the sirens in the distance getting closer to their house.

Shia couldn't stop searching the house. She heard the police come and heard Trent give an accounting of what happened;

still she searched. Her mind wouldn't let her grasp that her little girl was missing, not her baby.

"I'm going out to look for her." Shia suddenly announced as she grabbed her purse and keys off the kitchen island.

"No." Trent put his hand on hers and took the car keys. "The police said we should wait here in case she comes back."

Shia closed her eyes in an attempt not to curse her beloved husband out.

"Baby, I have to. I cannot sit here and do nothing. I just can't." She sobbed while a fresh wave of tears escaped her eyes. "Imagine how afraid Luna must be. I can't be without my baby," she wiped her eyes abruptly, pulling spare keys out of her purse.

"Either you're coming with me or you're not. What's it gonna be?" Shia gave him a pointed look speaking in a no nonsense tone.

"I will come with you." Trent told her as he removed the spare keys from her hand, "And I'm driving. Let's go."

Trent glanced at the twins, "Boys you guys are in change. Lock up the house and put on the alarm. We'll be back."

Trent turned to follow Shia out the house as they went in search of Luna.

****

Phylicia glanced at the sleeping toddler on the floor of her car with a warm quilt covering her up, while formulating a plan in her head as she began making the drive back to Greensboro.

CHAPTER 3

Elliot's heart lay heavy in his chest as he laid a single white rose on top of his wife's, Katherine, casket. Bending his head down, a tear slowly descended his pained face, trailing past his chin, lightly dropping on the stark white casket, his wife's new home, which gleamed bright in contrast to the darkness looming around him and the three other white caskets, which had become the new dwelling place of his children as well.

Grief stricken, Elliott felt as if his life was spiraling out of control. He stepped away from the caskets watching as the funeral staff began lowering his family into the ground.

Mourners and well-wishers were long gone. Elliott stood alone in solitude, hating to leave his family behind; he waited until the last casket holding his three-year-old son was covered by dirt. Unaware of the storm clouds looming, Elliott sunk to the ground on his knees and bowed his head. There was nowhere for him to go. He couldn't return to a house with no one in it.

No wife to greet him and ask him how his day was going or have dinner laid out on the table for him. No children to run up to him and say, "I love you, Daddy." Nothing awaited him there except an empty home; full of painful silence.

"Excuse me, Sir?"

Elliott raised his head to make eye contact with the Funeral Director with sadness in his eyes.

"We have to close up and lock the grounds gate for the evening. Will you be all right driving home? If not I can have one of my staff workers escort you."

Elliott slowly made his way to his feet without looking back at the place of his family's new home. He nodded toward the

Funeral Director as he began making his way to his truck; headed to an empty house, full of memories and regret for a life that would never be the same again.

****

Tick, tick, tick went the clock as Elliott tried to sleep in the California King he was used to sharing with his wife Katherine. He laid on his back with one arm propped behind his head as blood shot red eyes stared at the ceiling fan that was creaking softly as it rotated above him, torturing him with the steady sound.

The last few days had been hell on earth and he was having a hard time coping. It was two weeks past time for Elliott to return to his office, but he couldn't seem to get a handle on his life. His house was exactly the way his wife had left it because he couldn't bring himself to touch anything in the fear that he would somehow begin to erase memories of her. He knew that he would never be able to live without traces of her around. He needed to bask in her presence always. He hadn't been able to have a restful sleep since the funeral and his body was feeling every minute that it missed. He needed Katherine. Sometimes when he closed his eyes and lay in their bed, he could feel her presence all around him. He missed her touch, her smell, the sound of her lyrical voice that used to put him and their children to sleep at night. Everything. He missed everything. Why did she have to ruin their life? He wondered.

Katherine had been his world. He would have done anything for her, so when he'd come home and found her smacking skin with his neighbor, he had gone berserk. Not his Katherine. His queen. However, it was definitely Katherine laying in their bed head down, ass up, being long stroked.

Reliving it in his mind caused the tears to slide down his face. He hadn't meant to kill her, but his rage had overridden his judgment. He remembered that he'd let the skin smacking continue. He'd graciously backed out the room unnoticed, returned to work, and purposely stayed late. Making a quick run to the drug store, he'd gone back to his office to call his neighbor Mike. He asked him to check on Katherine and the kids, who had just called him to see how long he was working that evening.

Telling Mike that Katherine had thought she saw someone snooping around the house and was nervous with the three children in the house; knowing that his overly concerned neighbor would jump at the opportunity to stop by Elliott's house so that he could see and please Elliott's wife.

Elliott walked to the front of his office to the reception desk. The bubbly receptionist in his office stayed until the last associate left for the evening. He always appreciated that, but more so on this day.

"Reagan, I will be in my office if you need me. I'm working late this evening."

"Thanks for letting me know Mr. Washington. If you need anything, I'll be here," she smiled up at him seductively.

"Thanks Reagan, you're the best." Elliott winked at her.

Reagan, with her, Gabrielle Union good looks, made direct eye contact back as she batted her eyes and licked her lips.

Elliott gave a half smile as he returned to his office and locked the door behind him. He knew he could have sex with Reagan if he wanted to, but he never had because he respected the vows he had taken with his wife…the same wife that hadn't given a second thought to her vows after eleven years of marriage and three amazing children.

Cutting the music on in his office, Elliott took off his suit and went in his office closet to retrieve his gym bag. Quickly downing his gym clothes and a knit hat, he slowly opened the window to his office and climbed out. Careful not to bring any attention to himself, he strolled down the street whistling as sweet tune as if he didn't have a care in the world.

Approaching his home a short while later because it was approximately three blocks from his job, Elliott began walking in the shadows of the trees so that it would be difficult for someone to see him. The majority of the lights in his house were off. Elliott had known that once Mike had come over, that it wouldn't take long to get things heated up between the two.

"With my babies in the house," he thought to himself. He

knew the children should be sleeping since it was after ten, but that still didn't make it a wise decision on his part.

Breaking the glass in the kitchen door above the knob Elliott opened the door from the inside and walked in. Cutting off the house alarm, he silently grabbed a knife from the kitchen drawer before he made his way up the stairs to the second level of the house.

Entering each of his little one's rooms, he leaned down and kissed them on the forehead before pressing the steel edge of the knife blade to each of their throats, watching as blood oozed out of their freshly opened wounds.

His tears fell loosely, he loved his children, but they were a product of the whore he'd married, which meant they weren't fit to live, just as she wasn't.

Tiptoeing to the master suite of the house, Elliott stood still when he reached the door; torturing himself as he was serenaded by the sound of Katherine and Mike's love making session. Leaning his head on the wall, he closed his eyes and flexed his fingers repeatedly over the handle of the knife, trying to find the will not to do what needed to be done. Knowing there was only one way out of his misery, he prayed that God would forgive him one day. Reaching to turn the knob, he halted upon realizing that the door was locked. At least she had enough sense to lock the door with my children in the house. He thought.

Retrieving the key from the top of the doorframe, he quickly inserted it into the keyhole. The door silently opened offering Elliott a candid view of Katherine's body gliding on top of Mike's at a slow rhythmic pace. Elliot wanted to regurgitate at the sight of pure ecstasy on Katherine's face, but he quietly shut the door and slipped into the room unnoticed. Crouching low to the floor, he slowly made his way to a side table in the suite and squatted beneath it, patiently waiting for them to finish.

Elliott's heart broke a million times over as the continued sounds of their passion, threatened to be his undoing. After what felt like an eternity of minutes passed, Elliott finally heard even breathing coming from his bed.

"You have to go before Elliott comes home."

Hearing Katherine's voice halted Elliott as he had been in the process of standing up.

"I'm not worried about him." Mike's deep baritone voice responded, "You need to be planning your exit strategy. When are you leaving him? I'm tired of having to sneak around every day."

"Come on baby. It's not that simple. He and I have a family. Elliott will never let me leave with his children," she began shaking her head, "It's not going to happen."

Mike stood up, "Well, you need to figure it out. And by that, I mean do it soon," he emphasized as he began putting his clothes on.

"I will baby. I promise. We'll figure something out." Katherine whined from the bed, gathering the sheets to her chest as she sat up.

Mike finished dressing and leaned down to touch his lips to Katherine's.

"Good. I love you. See you tomorrow. I'll let myself out. Go hit the shower before your husband gets home. I'd hate for him to smell me all over you. However, you never know. He may like the way you wear my scent." Mike winked at her before he turned and strolled out the bedroom door.

Elliott was thoroughly disgusted by what he'd just heard. Listening for the front door, he didn't move until he heard it click into place. Swiftly leaping to his feet, he quickly made his way to the bed.

Katherine's eyes widened when she saw the intruder in her bedroom and she opened her mouth wide to yell out.

"Screaming will serve you no purpose."

Elliott whispered as he knelt in front of her, pressing the knife blade into her thigh.

"Baby what?' Katherine began as she recognized her husband's voice.

"Shut up!" Elliott snapped in a menacing tone. "I saw Mike and everything else you two did. Did you think I wouldn't find out?'

"You're obviously delirious. You didn't see what you think you saw. Let me get dressed and we can talk about this."

Her comment enraged Elliott even more now.

"You think this is a joke?" He asked as he punched her in the face. "You're going to sit here and lie to my face?" Elliott whispered in her ear as he flicked his wrist slicing her thigh open.

Katherine began screaming as she felt her face begin to swell from the punch and the pain of the knife threatened to be her undoing. Elliott pressed his hand to her mouth to muffle the sound.

"This isn't a game, Kathy. Shut your mouth right now." He leaned in close to her face and stared into her tear-filled eyes. "I cannot have this type of betrayal. Do you understand?"

Katherine nodded yes, since he hadn't moved his hand away from her mouth.

"I love you and this will hurt me much more than it will hurt you, but you leave me no choice." Elliott moved his hand from her mouth and leaned down to capture her mouth into a final goodbye kiss, their tears mingling together as they descended their faces.

The hand holding the knife came to the back of Katherine's neck and as he continued kissing the love of his life, he jammed the knife into the back of her neck and continued kissing her as her body jerked under the blade. He pressed the knife further into the back of her neck until he could taste the blood that was coming from her mouth. Only then, did he break their kiss and watch as her eyes rolled back in her head. He held her until her body went limp from the blood leaving her body.

He stared at her until the life left her body. He felt the last breath she took and thanked God for the intimacy of the moment. There was something strangely erotic listening to a person take their last breath, he thought.

God, I love this woman. He thought as he laid Katherine's lifeless body on the soft bed and swiftly stood up. Knowing that he couldn't stay away from the office for much longer without someone realizing he had left, he knew he needed to put some pep in his step on the way back. Quickly rummaging through the drawers and closets, he took a few of Katherine's expensive jewelry items and any money that she had in her pockets. He went to his side of the bedroom and did the same, knocking over a lamp and throwing clothes around the floor as he made his way around wanting the house to be in complete disarray to seem as if there had been a burglary. Stuffing the items he was taking in his pockets, he quickly ran through the house, pushing over furniture, knocking things off walls until he returned to the kitchen and left the way he had entered, leaving the back door open.

Staying amongst the shadows for the three blocks it took him to get back to the office, Elliott climbed into his office window unnoticed and changed back into his business suit. As soon as he sat down, a light tap came at the door.

"Mr. Washington, are you busy?"

Elliott went to the door and unlocked it so that Reagan could enter, "No, I'm not busy;" he answered her as he retreated to his seat.

"Do you plan on staying at the office much longer? It's getting late and I get nervous about walking home so late at night."

"Actually, I'm wrapping up. I will be more than happy to offer you a ride if you like."

Reagan's face lit up. "Oh, I would love that. Thank you so much Mr. Washington. Let me just grab my things and I'll be ready to go."

"Take your time. I'll be up there. Once I shut everything down in here," he told her as she nodded her head and went back up the hall. Elliott couldn't believe his good fortune. He would make sure he spent the night with Reagan, thus making sure that his alibi was airtight. Reagan would defend him until the end of time. As far as she knew, he had been in the office with her all evening and then spent the night at her house having hot sex and he was going to make it a point to blow her mind and back out.

CHAPTER 4

"Hi, you must be Avionne."

Avionne glanced at the top of the dorm steps to where the voice had come from and saw a handsome man with almond-shaped eyes and a dimpled smile speaking to her. Reaching the top of the stairs a bit faster than necessary, Avionne moved her bag to the side, so that she could shake his hand.

"That may be who I am. Who are you?" She was already skeptical. Before her foster mother passed away, she had pre-warned her of the type of man she would come into contact with at school. The kind of man that would only want her for what she represented and what she could do for them. While she may not have been rich yet, she more than made up for it in brains. Avionne wasn't a fool though. She had read about her mother and all the things she had put herself through for a man and she was having none of that. If a man wanted her, he was going to be the one looking the fool, not vice versa.

He smiled again showing twin pairs of dimples on each side of his smile.

"Don't worry; I'm not trying to be a stalker or anything. You can relax," he laughed, "My sister Clara sent me down here to see if you had arrived."

Avionne blushed at her own ego-tripping. She figured it was safe to say that every man in the world was not out to get her with some ulterior motive. Clara was her roommate. The two women had exchanged numerous emails over the summer and Avionne was anxious to meet her. She had neglected to mention her brother was so fine though.

"My name is Quincy," he said, shaking her outstretched hand. "Clara said that she was expecting you at any moment, so I came out to see, and here you are." He grinned at her.

"Nice meeting you Quincy. Thank you for coming down and being my very own welcoming committee."

"No need to thank me. Come on in so you can meet Clara." Quincy walked into the room ahead of her.

"Clara, look who I found lurking outside."

Clara put the last of her clothes in the bottom drawer of the dresser, shut it, and stood to her feet. Wiping her hands on the back of her jeans, she stuck out her hand.

"Clara."

"Avionne." Avionne replied, shaking the hand extended to her, "But you can call me Avi if you like."

"I do like." Clara laughed, "Avionne seems a little stiff. No offense." She helped Avionne with her bag. "I hope you don' have a boyfriend. I'm anxious to hit up the parties and meet some hot guys."

Avionne laughed at how peppy and blunt Clara was. "No offense taken and no, I don't have a boyfriend."

"Oh goodie! Then I just know that we'll have loads of fun." Clara exclaimed.

"Ahem. I hate to interrupt the girl talk, but there is a guy in the room." Quincy announced.

"Not really." Clara informed him as she jumped up and put Quincy in a loose headlock, ruffling his hair.

"Hey, cut that out." Quincy told her as he laughed and effortlessly lifted Clara off the floor, unhooked his neck, and lightly tossed her on her bed.

Avionne laughed as the two of them joyously played together. Wondering what it would have been like to still have Khloe around, if they would have played so freely, and gotten along as well Clara and her brother.

"You two are hilarious." Avionne chimed.

"You need to respect your elders."

"Elder? Please! You have ten minutes on me." Clara quirked at Quincy.

"Older is older, baby sis. Don't be trying to downplay my age since your roommate is in the room."

Clara burst into laughter, as did Avionne and Quincy.

"It must be cool having a twin." Avionne said.

Quincy playfully mushed Clara on the back of her head. "I guess, but I would have been okay being any only child."

"Yeah, but then you wouldn't have had the pleasure of me in your life and you would have missed out on all my wonderfulness." Clara quickly retorted.

"Girl, get out of here. The only thing I miss is having a normal quiet and peaceful life." Quincy stated as he turned to see Avionne staring at them.

"Sorry Avionne, we do this all the time. Please, don't mind us."

"I don't mind. It reminds me of home." Avionne replied as she began to unpack her clothes and think of Kamilah whom she hadn't spoken with or heard from since she'd rushed to pack her things and left home.

"I'm about to make a food run. You two want anything?"
Clara asked

"That's very abrupt and random." Quincy pointed out, "but
no, I'm good."

"Me too." Avionne responded.

"Okay. I'll be back." Clara said, looking over at Quincy.
"And Avi, watch out for my brother. He can be a handful."

Avionne laughed, "Oh, I can handle my own. Trust me."

"Clara, stop embarrassing me and go get your food. She will
be fine. I promise not to pounce on her. She's a big girl, she can
handle little ole me." He laughed winking at her.

"Yeah, yeah." Clara laughed as she exited the room.

"Your sister doesn't trust you alone with women, huh?"
Avionne asked Quincy once Clara had left.

"Don't mind her, she's only playing. She likes to think I'm a
baby even though she knows I'm not."

Avionne didn't see anything baby like about Quincy.
Standing at about five-nine, with shoulder length jet-black hair,
and an athletic physique, with creamy white skin he reminded

her of a fair-skinned Bradley Cooper. She definitely saw no baby. Avionne typically didn't date, but she knew that she was going to have to watch herself around Quincy. She was already beginning to lust after her roommate's brother and she hadn't been on campus a full day yet. She shook her head to get her mind right and got back to the business of unpacking.

Quincy watched silently as Avionne unpacked her things. He wanted to offer his assistance, but was tongue-tied. He had known Clara was going to have a roommate, but he never expected that one would look as good as Avionne did. Without Clara here as a buffer, Quincy didn't know what to do or say. It wasn't often that he was at a loss for words. Avionne was a pretty girl without the pretty girl attitude, which he appreciated. He could tell that Avionne's mother had raised her right and he'd be lying if he said that he didn't want a piece. His mother had also raised him right and as sexy as she was, he was going to take his time pursuing her.

Avionne could feel Quincy giving her the once over. She glanced up at him and caught him in the act. She could see a faint blush on his pale skin.

"So do you go here as well?" Avionne asked him, wanting to ease his obvious discomfort.

Quincy's skin was visibly flushed; he couldn't believe Avionne had caught him staring at her red-handed.

"Yes. I go here too," he told her.

Avionne was thrown off when Quincy suddenly jumped up and moved towards the door.

"Hey," she said, standing also, "Are you okay?"

"Yes, I'm just, I'm just…" Quincy began to stutter as Avionne came and stood directly in front of him.

"You're just feeling what I'm feeling?" She asked, raising her eyebrow and staring into his bright blue eyes. Without taking another second to think, she slowly stood on tiptoe and brought his head to hers to capture his full lips into a kiss.

Avionne allowed herself to melt in his arms for a second and then her brain began working again and she just as abruptly pushed him away. There was no way she wanted him to have the impression that she was easy or going to be one of his groupies. If he wanted any more kisses from her, he was going to have to earn them.

Quincy stepped back, "Sorry. Did I do something wrong?" He asked as he gazed into her eyes.

"No, no." Avionne flushed bright red, "We just shouldn't have done that. I, uh, I, uh," she stammered, "I can't do things like this," she broke his gaze.

Quincy nodded his head. He could take a hint. He didn't know what to think now. One minute he was enjoying a kiss, then the next she was pushing him away. Shaking his head confused, he left the room.

****

Classes were kicking Avionne's butt. She was a good student, but nothing could have prepared her for this. She thought undergrad had been a bit much, but nothing compared to law school. This level of study was much more intense. She rarely made time to go out. Unlike her roommate Clara, who hit every party that was thrown on campus.

"Avi, we're about to go grab something to eat at the Pub, you coming?" Clara asked her as she ran up to her in the hall.

Avionne wanted to head straight to the library, but she never hung out with her roomie because she was studying, so just this once she wanted to hang out.

"I'm in."

"Awesome! Meet you out in front of our dorm in about ten."

The Pub was a trendy spot near campus for college students to unwind. A majority of the students hung there Wednesday through Sunday night. College life was crazy like that even at the graduate level. Party all night, go to class, and study by day.

Avionne was feeling good as she and Clara entered the Pub. She saw Quincy holding down her and Clara's regular table so they began making their way to where Quincy was.

Quincy watched as Avionne and Clara walked over to him. Out of all the women there, Avionne was the only woman that mattered anyway, but once rejected, he wouldn't pursue her; she was going to have to come to him.

"Hey squirrel," Quincy said when she and Clara finally made it to the table. Calling Avionne the nickname he had thrown on her.

"Hey," Avionne replied as she and Clara sat down. She hated the pet name that Quincy had given her. That was a bad sign. It meant that he was thinking of her more like a sister than his woman.

"Hi Quincy." A team of law groupies sang in unison as they passed the table.

"Geez, it's like we're not even standing here Avi." Clara said, "These fast chicks be on twenty when you in here Q."

"I don't pay them no mind. They're only interested in two things," Quincy said, stopping to take a sip of water before continuing, "What I can do for them, and how they can make me give them what they want. I need a woman on her own grind."

Avionne smiled when Quincy said that. It was refreshing to see a man have more on the brain than sex. It proved he wasn't shallow and caught up in the hype. She wondered why he hadn't made another play for her since that day they first met.

"Hi Quincy." A seductively soft and husky voice spoke.

Quincy glanced up as a pretty, caramel sun dipped complexion woman with silky jet-black shoulder length hair approached. He'd be lying if he said he wasn't mesmerized. She reminded him of a tan version of Megan Fox.

"Hey," he said to the unknown girl. His gaze caught in hers.

"I'm Charlene," she replied as she stared into his eyes.

"Quincy," he said by habit, even though she had called him by name.

"I know who you are." Charlene replied smiling down at him. "The problem is you don't know who I am," She paused, "Yet, but you will," she said as she winked at him before walking away.

"Can you believe her audacity?" Avionne asked in disgust as she glanced at Quincy, but she may as well have been talking to herself. Quincy only had eyes for Charlene as he was now standing up, trying to keep her in his line of vision and Clara was engaged in conversation with one of their fellow classmates.

"I'll be right back." Quincy said, not hearing Avionne's question. He was on a hunt to speak more in-depth with Charlene.

Avionne sat at the table confused by what had just happened. She watched as Quincy caught up with the Charlene girl and escorted her to a corner talking to her. Jealousy was rearing its ugly head and Avionne didn't like it one bit. She wasn't known for being the jealous type, but this was the first girl Quincy had shown an interest in, which had her worried. I guess that's the kind of girls that he's into. She thought to herself as she kept an eye on the two of them in deep conversation for the rest of the night.

CHAPTER 5

Carrying the little girl into the house, Phylicia marveled at her flawless features as she gazed at the small bundle sleeping peacefully in her arms. Feeling a small pang in her heart, she had forgotten what this felt like. It had been so long since she'd held her own children in her arms. She realized she missed this feeling. A memory of Khloe presented itself and for a split second, she allowed herself to feel remorse for what she had done to her baby girl. Gently kissing the toddler's forehead, she was going to make sure that the same mishap didn't befall this one.

Early the next morning, Phylicia stood at the stove contemplating on what she should fix her little permanent houseguest. The cabinets were full of snacks and treats, but she wanted the little one to put something of substance into her system. After searching around the kitchen for another ten minutes, Phylicia decided on French toast and a fruit medley. Setting the food, plates, and napkins on the table, she grabbed a Dora the Explorer cup from the cabinet and poured milk into it.

"Where's mommy?" A sleepy high-pitched voice asked from behind her.

Phylicia turned to gaze at the toddler in her animal print pajamas. Placing the cup of milk on the oak kitchen table, she knelt down so that she could be eye level with the tiny tot.

"Your mommy had to go on vacation for a while, so I'll be your new mommy."

The miniature-sized person in her kitchen eyed her suspiciously, "No, I want my mommy," she stated calmly, while looking around Phylicia to see if her mother was behind the unfamiliar woman in the kitchen.

Phylicia gently touched her hand as she forced the little one's attention back to her. "She's not here. Now listen to me carefully, she may stay on vacation forever, and I'll be your mommy." She reiterated to the little girl.

"NO!" The toddler screeched as tears welled up in her big brown eyes.

Phylicia gradually tightened her grip on her hand, until the screeching ended abruptly and only tears flowed.

"You stop that crying right now. I don't have time for this." An exasperated Phylicia stood to her feet and scooped the girl into her arms at the same time walking her to the table, placing her in a chair so that she could eat her breakfast.

Sitting across from her, Phylicia eyed the stubborn toddler warily as she refused to eat from her plate. Phylicia ate her food in silence as the pint-sized toddler sat with her adult-sized attitude. Smirking, Phylicia respected her little spirit. Even at three, the girl refused to be pushed into doing something that she didn't want to do. Finishing her food, Phylicia stood, picking up her plate and cup to wash them. When she turned her back to face the sink, she smiled when she heard a fork scraping the plate. Stubborn or not, Phylicia knew that the little miss would get hungry at some point and would not be able to resist the food sitting in front of her face.

"May I have some more bread please?"

Hands and elbows deep in suds, "You sure may." Phylicia answered, grabbing a dishtowel to dry her hands.

"Is it good?" Phylicia asked as she placed another piece of French toast on the Elmo pictured plate.

The little girl ignored her question as she delved into her toast.

Phylicia shook her head and turned back towards the sink to continue washing dishes. She wasn't in the least bit worried, the two of them would be coming to an understanding soon enough.

"By the way, I'm going to call you Aleia, okay? You will answer to this name. It'll be as if you're a princess every day. You like that idea?" Hearing no response to her question after a moment of silence, Phylicia turned to stare at the child who was munching on her food, pretending not to have heard her question.

Finally having enough, Phylicia swiftly left the sink and marched up to the little girl pulling her out of her chair, the girls fork flying across the room hitting the wall from the quick motion. Phylicia was too angry to care at the moment; she was not in the mood to argue with a three year old.

"Listen to me, when I speak to you, you are to respond and this is the only time I'm going to tell you this. Do you understand? She yelled as a wide-eyed Aleia nodded in fear.

Phylicia smiled then kissed her cheek. "I'm so glad that we understand one another. Now finish eating your food so we can go out and get some items for your new room okay."

"Okay." Aleia responded mildly as Phylicia placed her back in her chair and got her a new fork so that she could finish eating her breakfast and she could finish the dishes, and the two of them could officially get the day started.

CHAPTER 6

The crisp morning air of the countryside was a welcome sign of fall. Ever since Elliott had relocated to North Carolina, he'd been working on putting the tragedy of his job and family behind him. Now in the south, he was hoping to make a brand-new start for himself and was relishing in the hopes of things to come.

After the situation with his wife and children, Elliott had been the prime suspect in the homicide investigation. Luckily, for him, Reagan had come through as an airtight alibi, just as he had known she would. Neighbors had reported seeing Mike at the scene of the crime and the detectives had found bits and pieces of Katherine's jewelry randomly scattered on his lawn as if dropped by mistake for someone who was in a hurry. Now Mike was behind bars for what the prosecution deemed an open and shut case to which the judge and jury agreed. He'd been charged with four counts of 2nd degree murder, sentenced to one hundred and sixty years in jail with no promise of parole.

Elliott smirked just thinking about it. The cops, detectives, lawyers, and judges were all stupid. He thought. If he'd known he could commit murder and get away with it so easily, who knows what he'd be doing with his life. Serial killer, maybe? He shrugged as the vision subsided and he pulled into the parking lot of his destination.

As he parked his truck, he realized that he was one of the first people at the Home Depot that morning. Pulling out his list, he made sure to pay attention to the things he really needed to get as he was fixing up a rambler that he'd bought in a short sale.

Making a beeline for the paint section, he was ready to get his home improvement projects underway. So anxious to choose his paint, that he didn't notice the woman standing with her small child in the middle of the paint aisle until it was too late.

"Oh, excuse me Ms." Elliott said as his hands shot out to steady the woman. "I didn't mean to run into you. My mind was a bit preoccupied." As he gazed down, he caught himself staring at the striking brown-skinned woman with the cute toddler who had her thumb in her mouth.

Quickly glancing away as she shot a pointed look at him, he felt his face flush hot while caught in the act. The unknown woman took in his demeanor with fiery interest in her eyes.

"It is quite alright," she responded, looking him up and down.

Elliott thought the woman standing in front of him with the little girl was very attractive. Her pose was beautiful. Phylicia smiled up at the man that she knew had unintentionally run into her at the Home Depot.

"I do apologize for not paying the attention. I should have been getting to where I was walking.

"I appreciate the apology." Phylicia responded as she looked up into his dark espresso brown eyes.

"Elliott Washington," he introduced himself while extending his hand for her to shake.

"Shayna Reynolds." Phylicia responded with her alias as she took his hand into hers and welcomed his firm grip before pulling her hand out of his.

"Is this pretty little girl, your daughter?" He asked her observing the toddler hiding underneath her sun hat.

"Yes, but she's a bit shy. Nothing like her mother," Phylicia made sure to add before glancing down. "Say hello Aleia."

"Hello." A soft voice whispered without looking up at Elliott.

He smiled a look of understanding at Phylicia. "Reminds me of when I had children." Elliott instantly regretted his statement, "Will you accompany me to dinner sometime in the foreseeable future?" He asked Shayna, quickly diverting the conversation hoping that would take her attention away from the statement he had just made.

"I would love that." Phylicia smiled, not in the least bit turned off or shocked by his forwardness. "But only if my little girl can come. I just relocated to this area and I don't really know anyone yet. I'm uncomfortable about calling a babysitting agency and leaving her with just anyone so soon after us moving."

Elliott smiled warmly at her. "Absolutely, it is okay. I completely understand. Since you'll have the little one, how about an early dinner around five and then we go hang out at the playground?"

Sounds like a date made in heaven." Phylicia said as she returned his smile. Pulling out a business card for her law consulting company, she handed it to him.

"Call me and we'll arrange the details."

"Will do." Elliott presented his hand to her again. "It was a pleasure."

"Oh yes, it definitely was." Phylicia stated with a hint of seductiveness in her tone as she held onto Elliott's hand a little longer than necessary.

Elliott retreated from the duo to handle his own home projects. Phylicia held tight to Aleia's hand as they continued searching for paint to decorate Aleia's brand new bedroom. While taking in the paint colors, Phylicia allowed her mind to roam back to Elliott Washington. From what she could recall, he seemed to stand about five-ten, and was a nice chocolate brown with pearly white teeth. He seemed to have a nice personality and Phylicia was looking forward to the date. It had been much too long since she'd felt a man's embrace and it was long overdue.

CHAPTER 7

Shia was beside herself with worry, frantically trying to keep busy and control her emotions. With the kidnapping of Luna, she hadn't been able to eat, sleep, or focus.

"Shy, you're really going to have to relax a little bit." Leigh exclaimed.

"Says the woman with no children." Shia responded sarcastically shaking her head. "This is outside of your expertise, so I would appreciate it if you kept all comments to yourself unless you are helping the situation."

Leigh frowned her face up at Shia's brash tone. "I thought I was helping you Evilena, but your attitude is very stank lately and I don't care for it at all."

"You know something, I can care less what you care for Leigh. Why not try leaving me alone. You're getting on my nerves."

Leigh opted not to say anything. If anyone was getting on any nerves around the house, it was definitely Shia with her negative energy. Her other children even chose not to be around her. The only person in the house who could stand her was her husband.

Leaving Shia in the living room in her state of evilness, Leigh began searching the house for Trent.

"You have got to speak to your wife. That heifa has gotten rude and mean. I don't even know my own sister anymore." She announced when she found Trent and the children hiding out in the basement.

"Yeah," Trent said, looking up from their sixty-inch LCD television mounted above the fireplace, unsurprised. "She hasn't been the easiest person to be around lately."

"I've never seen her like this. I'm, worried about her."

Trent looked at the sadness in Leigh's face. It was so much like looking into Shia's face since they were mirrors of one another, His own heart was sad.

"I'll go up and speak with her," he informed a concerned Leigh. Swiftly standing up from the plush black suede sofa, he jogged up the basement steps, and found Shia sitting in the family room on the chocolate sofa staring at the beige wall.

"Hey baby." He spoke cautiously. Shia's temperament these days was representative of a firecracker. "How are you feeling?"

"I'm not. I don't feel anything anymore. I just live."

Trent took in her forlorn expression and saw pieces of his old Shia dying. Taking a knee to the floor in front of her, he grabbed her hand and stared into her eyes; hoping for a glimpse of the fun, youthful girl he'd met and married years prior. His eyes searched hers hopeful, but the woman staring back at him expression fell flat.

"Hey." He spoke softly, "We're going to find her. Luna will come back to us I promise you."

"You don't know that." Shia's eyes watered, "We haven't even been able to find Phylicia in over a decade, and you think we'll find Luna in a few days? That's almost comedy at this point."

Trent released Shia's hand, "Well your negative attitude isn't helping anything."

"Excuse me?" Shia snapped as Trent's unsolicited statement broke through her daze. "What exactly is that supposed to mean?" Shia narrowed her eyes at him and his nerve.

Trent shook his head and stood up. His wife was looking for a fight and he wasn't in the mood to entertain her today.

"Nothing. I'll be back to check on you later." Trent told her as he grabbed his car keys from the key hook and left the house. Being around Shia was beginning to suffocate him and he needed to breathe clean, crisp oxygen, away from her negatively charged polluted air.

Shia watched him through the window as he left her spirit in turmoil. There was no doubt that she loved her husband, but the life she was currently living was costing Shia her sanity and she couldn't help but to suspect Trent was the reason.

"Hey."

Shia turned around as a soft-spoken Remi entered the room.

"Hey Rem." She solemnly responded as she leaned back on the sofa and closed her eyes.

"How are you feeling?" Remi asked as she sat down next to Shia and ran her fingers down the side of her hair.

"Like I want to leave this world behind. I miss my little Luna so much."

"I know you do honey and the same way you're missing her, I'm sure she's missing you just as much."

"Want to hear something crazy?" Shia began, "I don't want her to miss me because that will make her sad and I don't want her to be sad."

Remi nodded slowly, "I can see your point there, so let's talk about you and your sadness." Remi observed as tears escaped Shia's eyes.

"I'm so torn up, Rem. I'm dying inside. No parent should have to go through this. Haven't I endured enough?"

"As long as you breathe air into your lungs, you are going to go through trials." Remi paused in speaking, "I believe you're the one that taught me that."

Shia sighed, not in the mood for a walk down memory lane. "Thank you, Victoria Osteen. Remi isn't there something else you can be doing or somewhere else you can go?" Shia asked her wanting more than anything to be left in peace.

"Yup, right here with you."

"Great." A frustrated Shia replied.

"You know, you can't sit in here forever. Why not go spend some time with your kids? I'm sure they are missing quality time with their mama."

"They have both of their aunties here. I'm sure they'll be fine."

"True, but that's not the same as having their mom. They are not me and Leigh's children. They need you."

"Seriously." Shia retorted, "I love how you non-mothers are trying to tell me what to do with my own kids. Please go away and leave me be. I choose not to be bothered by anyone right now."

Remi sucked her teeth, "You keep this up, and you're going to end up alone. Then you really won't have to worry about anyone bothering you at all. We all understand that you are going through something, but that doesn't give you the right to disappear on your family when you're sitting right here with us. We know that you miss Luna. Her not being here affects all of us, but what about everyone living right here under this roof with you? None of us deserves the crappy attitude you've been dishing out. Contrary to whatever dysfunction is happening in your brain, your children need their mother back. It doesn't mean you miss Luna any less if you pay attention to them. For their sake, try to get it together. It's hard to explain to them when they ask, "Why doesn't mom love us anymore?" Remi gave Shia a pointed look as she saw her struggling to hold back tears.

"Of course I love them. They're all my babies." Shia whispered.

"I know you do." Remi responded lightly, "But they are children. You have to tell them by showing them and being around. You can't stay sitting on this couch staring at the wall forever."

Shia looked at her baby sister in a new light. She was being the mature one and for the first time, and Shia realized that she wasn't a kid anymore. Remi was right, but as much as she wanted to be their mom again, she couldn't. There was nothing left inside of her to give. No good night hugs, no kisses, or lazy afternoon storytelling sessions. Not one thing. She was tired of this life with Trent. She was tired of everything.

"Please let me be alone, Remi. I'm done talking to you about this. Actually, I'm done, period. Good night." Shia slowly stood up and went to her room, shutting the door silently behind her.

CHAPTER 8

Pulling up to Shayla's house in a black Tahoe, Elliott was excited about his date tonight.

Even though he'd sworn off women since Katherine, something about Shayla made him want to know everything about her. Stepping down from the truck in Tru Religion jeans, a button down, and a black sport jacket, he was ready to get the evening started.

Phylicia and Aleia greeted Elliott at the front door looking like a million bucks. Known for her love of Michael Kors, Phylicia had on a black cocktail length Paisley-Lace A-Line Dress, with her tinted black MK sunglasses, and a floppy hat on to block the sun and her face to keep people from recognizing her while she was out. She had little Miss Aleia dressed in a Burberry Ruffle-Shoulder Check Dress with white socks and patent leather shoes. She too had on a hat to shade her head and eyes as well as a tiny pair of sunglasses to shield her face from the nosey people.

"Wow Shayla, you look amazing." Elliott told her with a smile. "You do as well gorgeous," he said addressing Aleia.

"Thank you, Elliott. You clean up nicely yourself." Phylicia had to admit to herself that he did.

"Thank you," he told her as he led the way to his truck making sure to open the door for both ladies. "Is your daughter required to have a car seat?"

"No." Phylicia responded, "She's fine as long as she buckles in. Right, Aleia?"

There was no response. Phylicia turned in her seat to see that Elliott had already strapped the little girl in and she was sucking on her thumb ignoring Phylicia.

Aleia had Phylicia rethinking this whole motherhood thing. The girl never said anything; she never wanted to play and had yet to call her mommy. It was all starting to grind on Phylicia's nerves and she contemplated if she still wanted to be bothered with her or not.

"How was your day today?"

"It was nice Mr. Washington. Very eventful. I do law consulting, online and this one case I am helping with at the moment is hilarious."

"You're a lawyer?"

"Not anymore." Phylicia told him, regretting letting him know that about her. The less people knew the better. "What about you? How was your day?"

"It's getting better as I drive." He told her with a smile.

Phylicia smiled. She loved a man that knew how to bring the charm. "Is that right?"

"That's right," he laughed as they pulled up to their destination and parked. "I hope that this restaurant is okay. I've never been here and wanted to try it out."

Phylicia glanced up at the restaurant called Table 16 that was located on Elm Street. "It looks good to me."

"Wonderful," he said as he unstrapped Aleia from her seat and placed her feet on the ground. Aleia immediately put her hand in his.

"Come on Aleia give me your hand." Phylicia commanded her when she saw her willingly give her hand to Elliott to hold.

"No," Aleia responded. Phylicia's eyes narrowed on the little girl, who she would have snatched up if Elliott hadn't been watching her so intently.

"It's okay. I've got her," he told Phylicia seeing her reaction when her daughter told her no.

Phylicia smiled tightly. "She seems to have taken to you."

"I have that effect on children." Elliott leaned in close to her so that he could whisper into her ear, "I hope to have that effect on you as well."

Phylicia laughed, "We'll see Mr. Washington. I'll keep you posted on that status."

"Please do." Elliott told her. "I like to be kept up to date on matters."

"Same here. Well informed is the only way to be." Phylicia agreed with him as the trio strolled into the restaurant; they were immediately seated thanks to Elliott's reservation.

"Thank you so much for bringing the two of us to dinner tonight." Phylicia told Elliott as they were eating their meal.

"The pleasure is all mine."

Phylicia smiled. "Are you from here, Elliott?"

"No. I'm from Virginia. I gravitated here after the loss of my family." Elliott was amazed at how easy it had been for that to roll off his tongue.

"Really?" Phylicia's curiosity peeked, "What happened to your family?"

"They were killed," he said nonchalantly.

"I'm sorry to hear that."

"Don't be. Sometimes these things happen."

Phylicia nodded her head in agreement. "Yes, they do, don't they?" She stated matter of factly undaunted.

The two finished their dinner in a comfortable discussion as they relaxed around one another enough to enjoy the other's company.

CHAPTER 9

She had been watching her for weeks now. This was her route. Leave class at 4:45pm. Stop by the library and study for two hours, stop by the cafeteria to grab a quick dinner before it closed at eight. Go to the gym for an hour and a half and then jog back to her apartment to get home by ten. Take a shower by 10:15, and then pull out books for more studying to be completed by midnight. Every day, same routine.

Avionne watched and waited through the trees. The adrenaline coursing through her veins when she finally saw Charlene making her way down the dirt path. Watching in wait, Avionne's gaze focused on Charlene's feet as she listened to the cadence of her feet hitting the ground at a strong steady pace. She suddenly lost her balance and flew face first into the grass.

Avionne smiled as she shot into motion.

"Hi, do you need help?"

Charlene's body jumped when she heard the female voice; then relaxed when she saw Avionne's face. "Oh thank goodness it's you. You never know what kind of serial killers could be lurking in these trees."

Avionne laughed. "I know right. You have to be more careful. Are you okay?"

"No." Charlene stated as she looked down at her ankle, which was beginning to swell. "I think my ankle is sprained. I'm not even sure what I tripped over."

"Yeah, I didn't see anything. Here, let me help you up."

Charlene placed her arm around Avionne's shoulders as Avionne bent down and lifted a ninety-six pound Charlene off the ground.

"Thank you so much for helping me, Avionne. I really appreciate this."

"Oh, it's no problem at all."

Charlene's brow furred, "Why are we going this way?" She asked as Avionne veered away from the path and into the woods.

"Shortcut." Avionne tried to reassure her.

Charlene was skeptical. "Really? I thought there was nothing back here, but more trees. Are you sure this is the right way?"

Avionne ignored her question as her strides got longer. She took Charlene deeper into the wooded area.

"I want to go back." Charlene stated as she began to panic.

"Ok. Maybe you're right." Avionne told her. "I think I took a wrong turn somewhere.

"Let me put you down for a second to rest my arm and then we'll head back."

"Okay." Charlene said worried. She was mad at herself for leaving her cell phone at the gym with the gym bag locked up in her locker. Quincy had warned her about that and now she had no phone to call for help for the two of them.

Charlene was so lost in her thoughts that she hadn't noticed Avionne slip away from her. Glancing frantically from side to side, she didn't know what to do.

"Avionne! Avionne, where are you? Are you okay?" Charlene was in full-blown panic mode when she heard the footsteps behind her. Forcing herself to push through the pain, she slowly stood up and turned around. Body relieved when she saw that it was Avionne.

"Oh, girl. You scared me."

"You should be scared."

"What?" Charlene asked, confused.

"You can't have him." Avionne told her with no traces of friendliness in her features.

"Have who? Why are you acting like this?"

"You can't have him." Avionne repeated louder this time as the huge rock, that she carried in her hand came down on Charlene's head. Avionne brought the rock down again and again until Charlene's screaming subdued.

"There is only one woman for him and that woman is me." Avionne said as she placed the rock in her bag. She took her shoes off and put them in her nap-sac. Removing Charlene's shoes, she put them on even though they didn't fit and began walking through the woods to begin her journey home before Clara noticed that she was missing.

****

The campus was in an uproar about the girl that had been found in the woods with the body severely decomposing and pieces missing due to the animals having their way with the corpse.

"I knew something wasn't right." Avionne consoled Quincy as he laid his head on her shoulder with tears in his eyes. "Who would do something like this to someone as special as Charlene?" Quincy continued. He was devastated. Clara observed her brother in pain. She knew that this was tearing him up on the inside and she couldn't say that she didn't blame him. This was a tragedy in every sense of the word.

"Q, I'm so sorry that this happened. Is there anything that I can do to make you feel better?" Clara asked him trying to help him find peace.

"Can you find me another one of her? She was perfect." Avionne's body tensed when he said that Charlene was perfect. She was ready for him to be over this.

"Something like this happened to me when I was younger. My sister was poisoned to death by my mother."

Clara and Quincy both turned bewildered eyes toward Avionne,

"Are you serious?" Clara asked her in astonishment. "How do you get over something like that?"

Avionne shrugged. I was seven at the time, so I don't remember too much about either of them. Lucky for me, so that there won't be any scar wounds."

"I feel so bad that you had to experience something like that when you were so young," Quincy chimed in.

Avionne smiled on the inside. She was happy to have his attention away from Charlene's rotting corpse.

"Because of that, I spent my childhood in different foster homes. Being snatched away when one family grew tired of me...it was exhausting, but I survived. That is the reason for sharing my story with the two of you."

"You're right. If you can survive that, we can definitely survive this." Quincy said, tears still visible in his eyes and his heart refusing not to hurt.

"I had no idea your childhood was anything like that. You truly are a survivor, Avionne."

"In the midst of all your trials, somehow you landed here at Yale Law making something of yourself.

"That is something that you should be very proud of," Clara said, "I think you are amazing. In case you didn't know." Claire smiled at her. "People like you inspire me to help as many people as I can. As a matter of fact, I'm entitled to a ten million dollar trust on my 21st birthday.

"If anything ever happens to me, I want you to receive it. That will be my gift to you. Your life has been hard enough."

"Oh no." Avionne gasped. I would rather not receive it. I would hate for anything bad to ever happen to you."

"Clara." Quincy interrupted. Do you hear yourself? Do you think that is a good idea? I mean I respect what Avi has been through as well, but ten million is a lot of money. You don't just hand it out like that."

Quincy's statement made Avionne's blood boil. Here she had done him a favor by getting rid of Charlene and he wasn't even a little grateful. Instead, he had his mind set on making sure she didn't receive any money. Where was the loyalty? She thought.

"Q, mind your business, okay. Don't be a jerk. She's standing right here. This is something that we can discuss later. You're just not yourself because of this whole Charlene thing." Quincy shut his mouth and didn't say another word. Maybe Clara was right and he didn't want to make Avionne feel any kind of way about anything.

Quincy could be quiet now Avionne thought, but the damage was already done. He'd said what he felt he needed to say and he meant every word of it.

CHAPTER 10

Trent didn't know where he was going, he just wanted to be as far away from his house and Shia as he could get. Shia was running around, wanting to be alone and Trent felt as if he were alone. Driving to a deserted parking lot, he pulled in and cut the engine. Leaning his head back on the headrest, he closed his eyes. He was missing his ace, Kodi. Sometimes, when life got too hard for him, he would go off by himself so that he could talk to his homeboy.

"Man K, I would give anything to have you here with me."

Trent felt moisture behind his eyes. He wasn't the crying kind, but every time he talked to his man Kodi, he seemed to get choked up. It seemed like only yesterday they'd been hanging out before Kodi killed himself.

"My life is all messed up. I know if you were here, you would help me get through this. Phylicia has run my whole life. She's ruined everything for me."

I always said leave Phylicia's crazy ass alone. Didn't I?

Trent smiled through his tears; he could hear Kodi's voice in his head.

"Yeah, you did and I never listened. I never could get that woman out my system. It's like she did some voodoo on me or something."

Ain't no voodoo that strong, T. Maybe she was the love of your life. Maybe that's why you could never let her go. You don't want to get her out your system.

"You think so? That would explain a lot. So what am I doing with Shia? Playing house? I love her too."

No one says you can't love more than one woman, T. Shia's a good girl. Phylicia is bad, but your heart must have chosen her a long time ago.

"She killed my daughter!"

And yet, here you are, still in love with her.

"Maybe I'm the one that needs to be admitted, K."

Yeah T, cause Phylicia is crazy as hell.

Trent laughed. "You ain't never lied, K. You ain't never lied. How are they treating you up there? I miss you, bro." Trent told his boy as he sat in his car and talked to his fallen man as he did every time he needed his friend; he knew that he was the only one that could understand.

****

Trent was on the road to discovery. He needed to do some soul searching to figure out what was going on inside of him and how he was going to manage. He needed to know if he still had feelings for Phylicia or not. After all of the things that she had done to him and his family; the many ordeals that she had forced them to go through, he couldn't see himself still harboring feelings for her, but you never know. There had to be a something there... but what? He shook his head in frustration trying to figure out what was happening in his life. His marriage to Shia was on a downward spiral. The two of them couldn't see eye to eye on anything. He couldn't recall the last time that he had been intimate with his wife. She never allowed him to get close to her anymore. Even though they lived in the same house, they were becoming fast strangers. He missed her.

"Trent, can you please get your wife? She's downstairs being evil again. No one can take her lately. Why haven't you tried to get her out the house for a while? She's been holed up in here since Luna was kidnapped and she's sucking the life out of the other kids. It's depressing watching them walk around on eggshells because they're afraid of upsetting her."

Trent looked at Leigh and for one second wished that she were Shia. At least she was consistent. "You know your sister doesn't speak to me. I will have just as much luck getting her out the house as you would."

"Well, something has got to be done. She's annoying as hell. We're all completely over her. Make her go away." Leigh crossed her arms over her chest.

"I can't deal with her right now, Leigh. I'm sorry. You and Remi are going to have to take her out or just leave her down in the family room talking to herself. Just close the door so that the kids can do what they want to do."

Leigh shook her head. "Lord, I swear I wish that I could leave this place. I need a life outside of y'all's."

"See, now that's something you have to take up with God. So you called on the right name." Trent smiled at her.

Leigh laughed in spite of herself. "You're so crazy, Trent."

"Hey Trent, we have a baseball game today. Can you take us?" Ryder and Kyle came into the room, interrupting Leigh and Trent's conversation.

"Yeah, let me get my shoes on. Tell your sisters to get ready. We're all going to you guys game today to get some fresh air."

"Cool," they said in unison as they headed downstairs to round everyone up.

CHAPTER 11

"Does everyone understand the assignment?"

She, along with every other student in her class nodded yes to the professor's question.

"Good. See you all after the holiday."

Grabbing up her belongings, she sighed. Avionne especially hated this time of year. All of her fellow students would be going home to their families for the Thanksgiving break and she would be left on campus working since she had no family or home to go to.

Bouncing around foster homes for years after her mother had been sent to a psych ward for her delusional mind had left

Avionne an orphan, since her father was deceased. Year's back, when she'd been notified of her mother escaping the mental hospital, the little girl in her had waited and waited for her mother to seek her out, but that wish had been in vain. Her mother had never put in an effort to find her.

She didn't check on me one time, Avionne thought angrily as she headed toward the hallway exiting the classroom. Never even wondered if I was alive or dead and she doesn't care. The more Avionne thought about it, the more she resented her mother, Phylicia. No one person should have to endure the things that Avionne had gone through while growing up. Never having anywhere to call home or having the loving and nurturing touch of a mother, none of it. Avionne remembered growing up unsure of where her next meal was going to come from. She remembered hiding food under her pillows or blankets so she could make sure that she had something to eat for later just in case. Her foster mothers had all been mean to her with the exception of one, Ms. Krista. Avionne had loved her more than any words would allow her to express. The rest saw her as a monthly paycheck from the state. No one wanted to adopt her because she wasn't a baby. Avionne had made peace with that. However, she wasn't going to allow her early upbringing to dictate her future. In her first year of law school at Yale University on a scholarship, she felt as if she wasn't doing badly for herself at all. The one and only trait she'd inherited from her mother was love of the law.

Avionne's plan was to figure out a way that she could legally get back at her many foster mothers. They weren't going to get away with the way they had treated her. She was not going to allow that to slide in this or any other lifetime.

"Hey Avi, what do you have planned over the break?"

Avionne glanced up as Clara, one of her few friends at school spoke to her.

"Hey. Research and study."

"Girl, you need to loosen up." Clara laughed, "It's break time, so let's break. Why don't you come home with me and Q so we can have some fun?"

Avionne eyed Clara skeptically knowing firsthand that her reputation for being a party girl was completely accurate. Though she was nice as a piece of apple pie on a summer day, Avionne wondered why she had come to law school. Law didn't seem like the field, she should be studying. She seemed more of the free spirit, artistic type.

"Your fun and my fun are two complete, separate things." Avionne spoke gently trying not to hurt her feelings.

"I know." An undaunted Clara responded to her, "But that's the point. You need to learn to lighten up. Come to the wild side." Clara winked at Avionne. "Come on. It's one break." She told Avionne seeing that she needed more convincing. "A couple days out of your life, you get to hang with Q and me in the Hamptons. I mean what else do you have going on? You can always research and study when you get back. Trust me, learning is not going anywhere," she chuckled.

Avionne gave her a side eye and slow smile. It would be nice to have a real break; she thought, and enjoy a nice Thanksgiving meal.

"Okay." Avionne replied with much hesitation. "I'll go home with you."

"Totally awesome! We are going to have so much fun!" Clara exclaimed.

All Avionne could do was laugh as she watched the excitement on Clara's face.

****

Anxious to begin their school break, Avionne was taken back when they arrived at Clara and Quincy's home. Their family lived in Manhattan, but decided to spend Thanksgiving in East Hamptons this year. Avionne had never been to Long Island and especially not the Hamptons. She was elated that she had made the decision to accompany the twins' home for their break.

"Wow. This is nice."

"It's alright," Clara stated, throwing her navy blue 528i BMW into park. Not bothering to glance around the grounds, she wasn't impressed this was the lifestyle that she grew up in and was accustomed to.

"Okay." Clara began as she focused her piercing blue eyes on Avionne, reminding her of Rebecca Gayhart from the movie Urban Legend. "My mother is definitely OCD, so when you come in try to keep everything spic and span." Clara immediately offered up an explanation upon seeing Avionne's offended demeanor. "She yells at me and Q all of the time. I swear that lady has impossible standards." Clara shrugged, "Just wanted you to be aware. She's very uptight. Between you and me, I think she just needs to be laid. My dad has a mistress, I don't see why she doesn't go out and get someone and have an affair of her own."

"Seriously, Clara. Can you not expose all of our dirty laundry to Avionne? She doesn't want to hear about that sort of thing." Quincy interrupted sounding annoyed.

Avionne remained silent as she took it all in and let them hash out their battles. She marveled at how nonchalant Clara and Quincy both seemed to be about the whole thing and their matter of fact way of saying everything.

"Come on. Let's go." Clara said, throwing the car door open and jumping out. Quincy exited and disappeared somewhere onto the massive grounds before Avionne could get her door open good.

Avionne smiled as she exited the BMW a little slower. Clara's family home sat on land so elevated that Avionne could see almost the whole town beneath them. The grounds felt like a whimsical meadow that you could run through or lay in a hammock enjoying an afternoon nap. She had never been exposed to anything of this caliber before. She was impressed.

"Avi come on." Clara called down from the steps. "What are you waiting for?"

"I'm coming." Avionne yelled up at her bounding up the stairs to the back door.

Clara leaned in close to Avionne as she opened the kitchen door. "Remember, my mom is a special case. Don't let her get to you. Okay?" Without waiting for a response Clara stepped into the kitchen with Avionne on her heals.

"Hello, mother."

"Oh my Darling, you're home from school how marvelous. Who is your little friend?"

Clara's mom came over and patted her cheeks gently while holding a rocks glass in her hand. With her free hand, she reached for Avionne's hand.

"Mom, this is my classmate Avionne. Remember, I told you that she would be coming home with me for the break?"

"Oh, Avionne." She sang in a husky voice not quite looking her in her eyes. "Such a peculiar name, for a peculiar girl it seems. Please enjoy your stay at Wentworth Estate," she smiled softly as if in a daze as she retreated from the kitchen.

Clara smirked observing Avionne's bewildered expression. "I told you she can be a piece of work. Let's go. I'm a show you where you're going to stay."

"Ok. Lead the way." Avionne said as she followed her out of the kitchen.

****

That night, they went to a bar where they were partying it up and taking endless shots of Petron. "This is crazy fun." Avionne tried her best to shout over top the DJ mixing beats in the corner of the bar undetectable at first glance, because he was partially hidden by the stairs that led to the loft, which was the dance part of the bar.

"Oh my gosh!" Avionne screamed as a heavy weight crashed into her.

"So sorry." A drunken Clara slurred as she stumbled around trying her best to stand up straight.

"Clara maybe we should go. You're very inebriated and you don't need anything else to drink." Avionne looked around the bar trying to find Quincy until she spotted him engaged in lively chatter with another female.

"Don't be such a party pooper." Clara's discombobulated speech penetrated Avionne's hearing. "I'm just having fun." She told her draping her arms around Avionne's neck.

"A little too much fun, I think." Avionne told her. "Where are your car keys? There is no way that you can drive in this condition."

"Avi, calm down I'm not trying to drive, I'm just having fun." Clara sung, while still holding onto Avionne's neck as she took another shot to the head. "Uh oh, I don't feel so good." Clara announced right after she took the shot. Before Avionne could get her close to the restroom, the entire contents of Clara's stomach came out of her mouth and landed on her, Avionne and the floor.

Avionne was disgusted, but she didn't have time to focus on herself because Clara had passed out. Great, Avionne thought as she tried to hold up Clara's dead weight and fish for the car keys hidden in Clara's purse at the same time.

"Need some help?" One of the bar's security men asked her after they sent someone over to begin cleaning the floor.

"Yes, please." Avionne had never been as grateful as he picked up Clara and followed Avionne out of the bar towards the car, when Quincy suddenly appeared

"You all be safe, alright?" The security man told Avionne as he handed a passed out, snoring Clara to Quincy, who lowered her into the backseat as the two of them finished strapping her down.

"Will do and thank you again so much for your help." Avionne said as she started the engine and a drunken Quincy got in the car on the passenger's side. She started the engine and began driving towards Clara's family estate. As she pulled up to a stop sign, she began wondering if she was going the right way. She didn't see any of the landmarks she had seen when they had headed out to the bar earlier.

Hitting the accelerator when it was her turn to drive, she never saw it coming. One minute she was driving, the next minute something big and heavy collided with the BMW on the passenger and the world suddenly went dark.

CHAPTER 12

"Luna must feel so lost without her family." Leigh glanced up from her magazine at Shia's statement ready to say something smart, but then she saw Remi shaking her head warning her to keep quiet, so Leigh went back to reading her magazine opting not to say anything.

"I'm sure she does, Shy." Remi appeased her older sister because she knew that if she didn't, Shia and Leigh would be at each other's throats again today, and for the sake of the five children that remained, they needed some sort of peace.

Shia glanced over at Remi and smiled. Remi had really stepped it up. Her baby sister was a grown woman now and she appreciated that.

"Look what I found." Remi announced, holding up an old photo album. Shia's eyes lit up, while Leigh's gaze never deterred away from the magazine that she was reading.

"Oh, I want to see." Shia said as she stood to her feet and came to sit on the floor next to Remi. "Come on Leigh, come look. Where did you find this, Rem?"

Leigh sighed as she pushed her magazine aside. The two of them wanted to do some whole sister-bonding thing; she could see it in Remi's pleading expression. If she didn't want to strangle Shia and crush every bone in her body, she would be bent over laughing from Remi's facials. Leigh came to sit on the floor next to her sisters. She wasn't interested in going down memory lane. She liked her youth exactly where it was, in the past.

Once Leigh had taken a seat on the carpet with Shia and Remi, Remi gladly opened the album, coughing as a puff of dust reached out and attacked her nose.

"Achew." Remi sniffled.

"See, the album is even resisting." Leigh stated, "It doesn't want to be bothered either."

"Look at you two when you were babies." Remi exclaimed ignoring Leigh and her bad attitude.

"Haven't you seen this album before?" Leigh asked unfazed

"No. This is a different one. Not sure how I missed this one. It was in the few things that remained of Mommy and Daddy's," Shia responded.

"Oh." Leigh replied, shooting Shia a look.

Shia shrugged in response to Leigh's look and diverted her attention back to the album Remi was holding.

"You guys were so adorable. I wonder what happened." She giggled.

"We turned sexy." Shia shot back laughing, "You can't be sexy and adorable. We are the one that's more age appropriate."

"Lies you tell." Remi said. "I'm adorable and sexy. You better get your facts right," she laughed.

"You two are silly." Leigh smiled.

"Who is this woman standing next to Mommy?" Remi asked, pointing at a photograph that had the twins in separate strollers and a pretty woman standing in between them smiling.

Leigh looked at the picture and any trace of the smile she had just carried was gone. Shia glanced at Leigh then back at Remi, who was waiting for an answer, and made the decision to tell her the truth.

"Our mother." Shia answered.

"No, I see mommy, I'm talking about the other lady."

"I know who you're talking about." Shia nodded her head. "That woman is our biological mother; mommy's sister."

"What are you talking about, Shy?" Remi stared at her confused. "I don't understand what you mean."

"We're adopting, Rem, Sheesh. You're smarter than this. Catch up already." Leigh informed her.

"We cannot be adopted. I'm not ready to be adopted."

"Girl, you are in your thirties. You can handle it."

"How long have you two known about this?"

Shia shrugged, "Years ago."

Remi pushed the album to the side, no longer interested in going down memory lane. "And both of you conveniently," She held her hands up on quotes, "forgot to tell me that this happened?"

The hurt in Remi's voice was apparent. Under normal circumstances, Shia would have jumped right up to mother her, but these weren't normal circumstances, and Shia wasn't mothering anyone. Remi was going to have to man up and take the news just as they'd had to do.

"We thought it best not to discuss it with you at the time. You had gone through a lot that year and we didn't want to add that burden to your load." Shia told her.

Leigh shrugged her shoulders, "Shit happens, Remi. It's life. Deal with it. It's over and done. We were all raised by the crazy lady and we survived. There have really been no need to go back and try to dissect through our childhood. Our mother died in the fire. End of discussion."

"Yeah, while she may not have been the best mother, I respect her for taking on the responsibility of three children because she didn't have to and we didn't hear her complain about it one time."

"Well, where is our real mother?"

Leigh sighed as she stood off the floor and went back to pick up her magazine. She didn't sign up to be a part of this discussion.

"She died a long time ago, Rem. Our mother liked to live that street life until the drugs and the street killed her. We may have our issues with how we grew up, but we are still better for not growing up with her, you know."

Remi was in shock.

"It is just what is. Sorry you had to find out like this, but there really is no reason to feel like you missed out on some better life, because you didn't. Mommy made sure we did just fine. She may have been plum crazy, but at least she was there to go through our lives with us and she did the best I guess she could do anyway."

"This is crazy." Remi whispered, "Being a member of this family is just too much for one body to take."

"Now that, I do agree with." Leigh said, pointing at her from across the room. "You just said a mouthful there, girl."

"I'm going to bed. I don't want to discuss this anymore."

"Okay." Shia responded, "And Rem." Remi turned to face Shia, "Don't let this consume you. Make peace with it and let it go. It's over and done. We can't go back and change time."

"I know Shia." Remi responded solemnly. "Good night."

"Well, I could have told you that was going to go badly." Leigh said to Shia.

"The girl deserved to know. She's grown now. No sense in lying to her."

Leigh sighed again and shook her head. "She was right about one thing though, being a member of this family is too much ALL the time."

"You won't get an argument out of me there, sister. No argument at all."

CHAPTER 13

Opening her eyes slowly, Avionne woke up with a massive headache. Staring up at the white ceiling, she focused on it trying to figure out where she was and why her whole body felt like it had been in a war and lost.

"You're awake." A sullen voice said to the right of her.

Avionne attempted to turn her head, but the pain was too severe for her to accomplish that small task.

"Don't try to move." The voice warned her as the sound came closer.

Avionne waited patiently for the voice to make their way into her line of vision. She was surprised when she recognized Clara's mother.

"Why?" Avionne managed to say her voice raspy from non-use.

Clara's mother stroked her hair soothingly.

"Why are you here you asking?"

Avionne went to nod and immediately stopped when the motion instantly brought tears to her eyes.

"Relax. Don't move too much. Your body has been through quite an ordeal."

"What happened?"

"You and Clara were in an accident. Hit by a drunk driver."

Avionne blinked rapidly trying to remember. "Clara passed out from all the drinks she had. We were on our way back to your house. Is she okay?"

Clara's mother shook her head no. "No, sweetie. Clara didn't survive the crash.

The pounding in Avionne's head got worse at the news as tears sprang to her eyes. Now things were beginning to make sense to her. No wonder Clara's mother was waiting in her hospital room. Avionne appreciated that she had been there for her since she had no family of her own.

"Thank you." Avionne told her as she began drifting back into sleep, "for not leaving me," she felt Clara's mother squeeze her hand as she slowly relinquished her hold on consciousness.

When Avionne woke the next morning, Clara's mother was sitting next to her bed knitting and sipping on a flask.

"Morning." Avionne managed to croak out.

Clara's mother looked up from her knitting. "Oh precious girl! It is evening time, darling," she stood up and walked up to Avionne's bed. "Are you thirsty?"

"Yes." Avionne responded afraid to nod even though the pounding in her head wasn't as harsh as the previous day.

Clara's mother gently propped Avionne up on the hospital pillows into a sitting position. She then brought a cup to her lips and Avionne was grateful for the cool liquid to hit her lips.

Clara's mother stood patiently, holding the cup until Avionne finished.

"Need some more?"

"No, ma'am." Avionne replied.

"Good. Now we can move on to business."

"Business?" Avionne asked confused, not understanding what kind of business she could possibly have with Clara's mother.

"Yes, business." Clara's mother sat back down in the chair next to Avionne. "It seems as if you made quite an impact on my princess Clara. So much so, that she left the trust given to her by her grandfather to you."

Avionne just stared at Clara's mother; she had no idea that Clara had a trust in her name.

"Clara would have received her trust on her twenty-first birthday, which passed while we were waiting for you to wake up, so now you are the beneficiary of Clara's ten million dollar trust."

If Avionne wasn't already lying in a hospital bed receiving medical attention she would have definitely needed it upon hearing Clara's mother statement.

"Are you serious?" Avionne asked in disbelief. "Why would she do that?"

"My daughter was a special girl. She was always seeking to help and make the world a better place anyway that she could." Clara's mother shrugged her shoulders, "She gets that from her father's side."

Avionne chose not to acknowledge Clara's mother's comment with a remark. There was no need. She now knew that if it were up to her, Avionne probably wouldn't be receiving a thing. However, Avionne was too elated to care either way. She was a millionaire!

CHAPTER 14

Returning to school after the unfortunate accident that had kept her in the hospital for over two months, she stared at the empty glass of vodka that she just sat on the table. Avionne sat in her dorm room, unable to believe her good fortune. She had done it and gotten away with it. No one suspected her. She was a free woman...ten million dollars richer and she was elated. Clara and Quincy's mother treated her like her own now. Avionne figured the loss of twins could do that to a person.

Twirling in circles around her room, she stopped to stare in the mirror at Phylicia stared back at her. So shocked she abruptly turned away from the mirror joy subsiding. She saw her mother's face when she glanced in the mirror. Is that who I'm becoming? She asked herself. Is that the type of person that she wanted to be? Was that what her whole life was beginning to be about?

Not that it mattered. If she turned out like her mother, it was only fair. Phylicia was the reason that she was the way she was and she had no problems blaming her mother.

She wasn't a complete carbon copy of her mother. Her feelings were hurt that she'd had to get rid of Quincy. That was chipping away at the core of her. Quincy was the first guy that she had really taken a liking to. She really wanted to see what direction things would go with him, but hadn't expected him to get so hung up on that Charlene girl. That had thrown a monkey wrench into everything that she was trying to do with him.

Avionne completely regretted killing Charlene now. If she would have known that Quincy was a complete douche bag, she would have let Charlene have him all to herself and the two of them could have run off into the sunset together. Avionne guessed that was something that the two of them could do together in heaven. She didn't care what they did now. They could have one another.

Glancing around her empty dorm room, she would be lying if she said that she didn't miss Clara's constant chatter. Clara was a different matter altogether. She loved that Clara genuinely cared about her. Outside of her foster mother Krista, Avionne didn't know how to care about other people. Her mindset was always, if your own mother didn't want you, no one in the world would want you either.

Sitting on her bed, Avionne recalled the night of the accident. The twins were friends with the bartender at the bar they had gone to. In celebration of their 21st birthday approaching, shots were in abundance that evening, even though they were all underage. Avionne had two shots and then made it a point not to have anymore. She never liked to be in a situation where she lost control, even for a moment. That just wasn't her style. She needed to remain alert and in control at all times. She had to know what was going on and why.

When Clara had thrown up on her and everyone within standing distance, Avionne had quickly taken her to the car. She wanted to allow Clara to try to sleep it off while they waited for Quincy to finish getting his party on. When they got to Clara's car, she noticed that Quincy was inside getting it on with a woman Avionne saw celebrating with them earlier in the bar. Avionne was livid. Kicking the car, Quincy looked up in amazement turning beet red.

"What are you doing?" Avionne yelled. "Your sister is in their losing her entire stomach and you're out here trying to get your rocks kicked by some hoe!"

The girl seeing the rage in Avionne's face opted not to say anything as she quickly fled the vehicle pulling her blouse down as she hightailed it back to the bar.

"What's wrong with Clara?" Quincy asked as he blatantly ignored Avionne's question.

"You're seriously going to act like that didn't just happen?"

"What are you talking about? You always seem to focus on the wrong things. What is going on with my sister?"

"She's drunk." Avionne replied with an attitude, "What does it look like. From the smell of things you're probably drunk as well."

"Don't worry about me. I can handle my own. Let's get Clara home," he took his sister out of the security man's arms and draped her body across the back seat."

"Get in the car. Let's go."

"Uh, negative. You are not driving me anywhere. You are drunk. I'll drive."

"Fine. Let's just go." Quincy told her unwilling to give Avionne the fight that she was looking for. In his drunken state, he stood to lose the verbal exchange anyway.

Avionne was happy that she won that small battle as she entered the driver's seat and Quincy sat on the passenger side. Not too long after they began the ride home, Avionne heard light snoring coming from the passenger's seat. Glancing over while stopped at the stop sign, not too far from the twins' home; she saw that Quincy had fallen asleep. Avionne shook her head at the both of them. That's why she didn't usually partake in any substances; be it alcohol or drugs. She always needed to be in control of her life.

Sitting at the stop sign, Avionne was about to drive forward when she saw a truck's headlights coming quickly in their direction. Acting quickly, she pulled the BMW right into the trucks path and braced herself for the impact. If she died tonight, she could handle that. She hated her life anyway, but if she lived and the twins died, she would be ten million dollars richer. She always wanted to know what it was like to be a millionaire, she thought as she heard screeching brakes and the truck plow directly into the passenger side of the BMW killing everyone on impact except for Avionne.

Isn't God good? Avionne thought as she glanced around her dorm room. I'm a millionaire. I'm a millionaire. She thought to herself as she flopped back on her bed and closed her eyes immediately drifting to sleep, her body long overdue for a nap.

CHAPTER 15

The campus library was deserted and Avionne couldn't have been more grateful since she seemed to be having a bad run of luck this morning. Her laptop was kaput after she accidentally dropped it on the hard floor as she maneuvered through the halls to her class today. Running behind schedule, she hadn't bothered with putting it in its case. Now she found herself in the library; she needed the internet and could not get the access any other way.

Typing the name Phylicia Taylor into the Google search engine, Avionne waited patiently for the results to appear. When the results appeared on the screen, Avionne noticed that the first link was that of the FBI's wanted list. Clicking on the image link, she was anxious to see the photos of her mother. The one thing Avionne did love about her mother was her features. It always amazed Avionne how much she resembled her psychotic mother. They had the same sparkling brown eyes, full hair, pouty lips, and brown skin tone.

She's so beautiful, Avionne thought staring at the pictures of Phylicia in the various photos that were available online. One of the photos was a shot of Avionne, Phylicia, and her little sister Khloe. Avionne rarely thought of Khloe. She died so long ago that it was hard to remember anything about her. Avionne later read that her mother poisoned Khloe. That news haunted her ever since she found out. By God's grace, her mother had spared her life and that was why she prayed every morning and every night. It was a miracle that she was even alive at all.

Avoinne returned her focus to discovering more information on her mother in hopes to get a feel of her whereabouts. Avionne could see her mother was still on the run. This meant finding her would be like locating a needle in a haystack, but find her she would. Avionne needed answers and come hell or high water, she was going to get them. Stopping by the registrar before she returned to her dorm room, Avionne figured the time was now or never. She was leaving law school. Time was of the essence now. She needed to find her mother. She could always come back and finish school, but it was time. The time had come for her and Phylicia to have some official mother-daughter time. Avionne felt that after thirteen years she deserved that. At the very least, she wanted an explanation for why things had gone the way they did. Why Phylicia had never sought Avionne out to check on her own daughter, her own flesh and blood.

While pursuing the internet research of her mother, Avionne was able to pull old news articles that gave useful information about her mother.

"Wedding Goes Up In Flames" Attorney at Law Phylicia Lynn Taylor makes headlines again. Only this time, it's with a grotesque account of how easy it is to fall from a life of luxury to a prison cell. Over the weekend, at a private wedding

ceremony in MD, where two unidentified New York State residents who were to be married, Ms. Taylor allegedly set ablaze the couple's wedding tent, also stabbing a security guard on duty - who was later pronounced dead. Ms. Taylor also is accused of injuring the groom. He was treated on the scene for minor injuries and released. We are happy to report that the lucky couple was able to exchange their vows and dedicate their undying love to one another. May they have a very "fiery union."

Avionne laughed at the reporter's sense of humor. She wasn't sure that if it were her wedding that she would have enjoyed the article with the same amount of merriment that she was displaying now.

There is no denying that my mother is truly a force to be reckoned with, Avionne thought to herself as she continued finding more and more stories about the things that her mother had done. Her past horrendous deeds superseded the many good things that she had done. Before she had met Trent, she had been a completely different person. She was always volunteering her time and services to help those in need. Her mother had been known for her ability to convince high society, individuals to donate massive amounts to numerous charities and causes. The media rarely, if ever focused on that side of her. That's the woman that Avionne wanted to remember of her mother. In her heart, she may be able to forgive that person. The woman that killed her child as well as numerous others and chased a man for two decades... that's the one that she was having a hard time forgiving.

She wanted to understand what was going on. She thought, "What could possibly make her have this completely obsessive attachment to that man Trent?" It was apparent that Phylicia had some form of a mental illness. She had broken out of the hospital years ago and no one had a clue of her whereabouts since then. Avionne was having a hard time gauging what mental state her mother would be in at this point.

How do I locate her? Avionne began thinking to herself. Suddenly, a light bulb went off in her head. I know if I can figure out Trent's location, I know my mother can't be too far away. She's obsessed.

Avionne pondered long and hard. She'd done her research and knew that Trent and his family were in protective custody, which meant that they were more than likely living under aliases. She sighed and tried to think of where she could gather information on his family. Sitting on her bed with her laptop, Avionne leaned back on the pillows and tried to think of something. Her memory was so vague from all those years ago. The one thing that she clearly remembered was Khloe's death. She remembered waiting at the hospital with Trent for her dad to arrive. She remembered him putting her in the car with twin boys that had to have been three years old at the time. Avionne sat up abruptly. She had completely forgotten about them. She had brothers! Blood flowing through her veins, she pulled up the website where she could contact the department of social services.

She knew that she was banking on a miracle. Yet she was hoping against all odds that they had kept her last known relatives on file. Writing down the address closest to her, which was about forty minutes away on Farmington Avenue in Connecticut. Avionne quickly glanced at the clock, which read fifteen minutes before noon. She had plenty of time to throw on some clothes, head down the DSS Office, and see what they could tell her, if anything.

****

Sitting and waiting for someone to help her, Avionne was agitated. For the life of her, she couldn't understand why it was taking so long to pull up her files.

"Does there seem to be a problem with my paperwork?" Avionne inquired of the woman seated behind the desk.

"No, ma'am. It's just taking a little bit more time than normal. We're waiting for the New York office to fax us some documents."

"Seriously?" Avionne asked the clerk with a hint of an attitude in her voice. "You mean to tell me that this office hasn't switched over to digital files yet? Are y'all working in the twilight zone? I mean, come on. This is ridiculous."

"Ma'am, you will have to wait." The clerk told her with her own attitude and turned her face back to her computer screen." Because this was a government building, Avionne decided to let the clerk get away with speaking to her in such a brash manner. She wasn't trying to go to jail today. Unlike her mother, she knew how to avoid jail time.

Thirty minutes later, after many evil glances to the clerk, she was finally presented with a copy of her file.

"Thank you for waiting so patiently." The clerk's voice oozed of sarcasm.

Avionne was so engrossed in the documents that had been handed to her; she was oblivious to the clerk's sarcasm. Much too anxious to wait until she returned to her dorm, she planned to delve into the massive paperwork to find out the contents of her file as soon as she made her way back to the car.

She quickly read through the documents until she got to the part about her last known relatives only to discover that the DSS office had marked through it with a sharpie. Avon squinted;

trying to make out the letters, but soon gave up not wanting to strain her eyes.

After returning to her dorm room, Avionne sat down at her laptop and entered *"how to remove black sharpie permanent marker from paper"* into the Google search engine. Finding a good recipe on ehow.com, Avionne followed the directions until the words began to show on the paper again. She could make out the Atlanta address and was able to make out her brothers names, Kyle and Ryder. Avionne dropped the paper and smiled. It was time to pay her long lost brothers a visit.

CHAPTER 16

She was bored. Sitting in her quiet country house, Phylicia couldn't believe how domesticated she had become. She was a far cry from the woman who used to love to chase Trent around and she missed that spirited girl. It wasn't as if she didn't love spending time with Elliott and Aleia, because she did, but she needed more excitement. She needed old Phylicia to come back and rescue her.

"Babe," she yelled, grabbing her car keys, "I'm going out for a bit. I'll be back." Not hearing a response back, Phylicia wrote Elliott a quick note and bounded into the car leaving him and Aleia indoors.

Sliding behind the wheel of her charcoal gray Volkswagen coupe, Phylicia sped away not letting up off the accelerator until she merged her way onto the highway 85 southbound toward Atlanta.

Five hours later, Phylicia breathed a sigh of relief when she saw the highway sign read 'Welcome to Georgia'. Finally! She thought. Times like this one she wished that she wasn't considered still on the run. "A plane ride would have made this little excursion so much better," she mumbled to herself.

Cutting her car lights off as she drove onto the street, she proceeded to park on the corner; she then quietly shut the car door and exited the vehicle.

Grateful that she had remembered to wear sneakers, Phylicia quickly ran among the shadows along the side of the houses until she reached the house she wanted. Kneeling beneath an open window, Phylicia shut her eyes and sighed at the sound of her beloved…the keeper of her soul. Her heart started to flutter as the voice serenaded her in the darkness. It was Trent.

Being as still as a predator seeking out their prey, the undetected figure watched the woman kneeling below the window with her eyes closed in disbelief. Squinting in the darkness, she willed her eyes to readjust so that she could get a clear view of the woman's face. She needed to verify that it was who she thought it was.

Shifting her head to the right, she saw the car housing the detail she assumed had been assigned for the inhabitants of the house protection. "Some detail!" she thought, as the men inside the car appeared to be sleeping. Snorting in disgust, she quickly realized her mistake when the woman under the window leapt to her feet.

Phylicia wasn't sure what made her jump up from her position under the window, but she had an eerie feeling that she was being watched. Observing the darkness around her and not seeing or hearing anything, she wondered if she had gotten paranoid over the years. Sitting under the window once more, Phylicia sat listening intently.

"I miss my baby." Shia sobbed. It had been nearly six months since her baby had been stolen right out of their front yard.

"I miss her too." Trent said.

"Oh really? I can't tell." Shia snapped at Trent.

"What is that supposed to mean?" Trent asked her.

"Exactly what I said."

Trent knew Shia wasn't herself lately, but her attitude everyday was beginning to irritate him.

"I may not show my hurt or feelings the way you do, but that doesn't mean that I don't miss her any less. She's my baby too, not just yours."

"You walk around here every day like things are normal and they are not!" Shia raised her voice slightly.

"That's because we have five other kids, both parents can't forget about them and not pay them any attention. One is enough. They need at least one of us to be functioning. While I miss Luna, I have to focus my energy on the ones that are still here."

Shia rolled her eyes. She and Trent had been at odds lately because she was tired of this drama-filled life that came with him.

"You treat me like you blame me." Trent continued.

"I do blame you okay! There I said it." Shia shouted extending her arms into the air.

"I blame you for this crazy life that our children and I have to live because of that crazy ex-girlfriend of yours. It's been over ten years of this. I mean it's too much for anybody to have to go through."

Trent found himself in disbelief, "I thought the two of us would be able to survive anything."

"I didn't know you felt like this." His feelings were hurt. If there was one thing Trent always banked on in life, it was that Shia would have his back and be in his corner forever. Her loyalty was now in question.

Shia hated to see Trent hurt, but after all these years she'd had enough. Her baby being snatched out of her front yard had been the final straw. She could barely breathe without knowing where her baby was, so Trent's feelings meant nothing to her now.

"I need some time away from you and this life. How about you leave for a little while? Give me some time to sort through all of this and clear my mind. Then, once some time has passed, we'll talk and figure out what we will do."

"If that's what you want. Fine, I'll leave tonight."

"Okay." Shia sighed as she left Trent in the family alone.

On the other side of the window, Phylicia smiled. After years of chasing down Trent, Phylicia was dumbstruck that Shia was handing him right to her. Now maybe they could have what they had before. She may even return his daughter to him under those circumstances.

Making her way back to her car, Phylicia waited patiently for Trent to come out of the house so that she could follow him to his destination.

Trent checked in at the Marriott down the street from his home on West Trade Street. He was beginning to question everything about his life. After all these years, maybe Shia wasn't the woman that he thought she was...maybe she truly wasn't the woman that he needed to be with. He could not fathom that after all these years together with him owning up to his responsibilities and providing for his family, she wanted to leave him over issues that were beyond his control. Hearing these new revelations from Shia changed his view of her completely. He understood that they were going through a lot as a family. However, not once in all these years had he ever thought about giving up on her. Not once did it ever cross his mind. Not once.

CHAPTER 17

Never in a million years would she have predicted this. The cards were negligent to not warn her of such a moment as this.

"Say it ain't so." Leigh sobbed walking into the kitchen.

Shia watched as her sister invaded her kitchen area with tears falling down her face and snot flailing everywhere. If the situation hadn't been so dire, the sight of Leigh would have made Shia laugh at the pure comedy of it all.

"I still can't believe he's gone Shy. I think that this is some cruel joke that is being played on all of us." Leigh cried as she draped her body across the kitchen island.

"I can't say that Lei Lei and why are you coming in here with all your theatrics?"

"Because this whole thing is very unfortunate." Remi interjected as she strolled into the kitchen. "Who would have thought after all these years you would actually leave Trent?"

"I know I didn't." Leigh wailed from on top of the island. "Shy, I usually stay out of you and Trent's business."

"Since when?" Shia asked sarcastically choosing to wash dishes instead of put them in the dishwasher.

"Okay, maybe never." Leigh admitter, "But don't you think you are carrying things a bit far this time? You put Trent out for no reason." Leigh studies Shia's face intently.

"Oh, there was definitely a reason."

"There was no real reason." Remi announced, "I think you're going through a midlife crisis or something. Cause you plumb crazy to leave a man like Trent! He would never have left you.

Ever. I hope you think about that when you sleep alone in that big ole bed at night. It's borderline betrayal. What kind of wife are you?"

Shia refused to let the two of them make her feel bad. "What is wrong with you two? Do you realize we are still living in hiding? Do you guys not get that? Because of his psycho ex, we've been living in hiding for years. Not only that, my baby is missing. Luna is gone! Or have y'all forgotten? Trent doesn't care about any of that. He's just walking around like everything is all sunshine and roses."

"We're not trying to upset you Shy, but did it ever occur to you, maybe he doesn't know how to show that he's hurting? I'm sure he hates that there is no way he can protect his family the right way and has to rely on law enforcement to do it." Leigh jumped down from the island and walked over to Shia, "I know he misses Luna. That was his baby as well. Has it crossed your mind that this is the second daughter he has lost? Just because he's not expressing his hurt and frustration the way you are, doesn't mean it's not killing him on the inside. He doesn't like this situation any more than you do, but he rides it out beside you every day of his life. Now that's a good man, Shia. You over there bugging! You need to get it together."

Shia stared at Leigh for a long time before dropping her head down and allowing the tears to flow. "Everything you said is true." She whispered aloud to her sisters. "I miss my husband and you're absolutely correct, I know he's hurting too." Shia wiped her face not caring about the detergent suds and water that ran down her face waltzing with her tears.

"I'll be back in a second." She said, leaving her sisters in the kitchen to find her purse in her bedroom in order to retrieve her cell phone. Sitting on the edge of her bed, she dialed a number and waited patiently as the phone rang. After five unanswered rings Shia was about to hit the end button when the line was suddenly picked up.

"Hi baby. I miss you." Trent's sleepy voice filled the line.

Shia closed her eyes as she allowed her husband's deep voice to soothe her ears. "I miss you too." She whispered, "Trent, I'm so sorry. I know that I've been impossible lately. It was selfish of me to take my feelings out on you by being completely inconsiderate of your feelings." Shia paused and Trent stayed silent waiting for her to continue.

"I've been a bad wife to my husband. Will you forgive me?"

"I love you more than my next breath." Trent finally spoke. "I would forgive you for anything a thousand times over. Don't you know that?"

Shia sighed, happy that her marriage was still intact. "I do know that."

"Why don't you come see me? Take a breather from that house for a little bit."

"What if someone brings Luna back and I'm not here?"

"They will call us, Shy. Please baby? Sitting there miserable is not going to make anything happen any faster. Come see your husband, he needs you." Trent told her seductively.

Shia could hear the sexually charged energy in her husband's tone. "Okay, I'll come. See you in a few my handsome husband."

"You got it, my beautiful wife."

Shia arrived at Trent's hotel room within the hour. She had on a trench coat, 6-inch Louboutin's, red lipstick, hair piled on top of her head in a loose bun, Chanel sunglasses and nothing else. Knocking on the door, she waited patiently for her husband to receive her.

Trent had the bubbles in the Jacuzzi ready, a tray of strawberries on the side, sparking wine in two glasses, music playing softly and the lights were dimmed as he anxiously anticipated the arrival of his wife.

Hearing a soft knock at the door, he glanced through the peephole and cracked the door open to let his guest slide. He wanted to make sure she had to brush up on his body as she passed.

"Looks like you're expecting company? Hope I'm not interrupting?" Trent watched as her words slide past red lips.

"You can always interrupt. I was only expecting my wife. She can wait."

Shia laughed, "Do women really fall for that line?"

"You tell me," Trent gazed down at her, "Did it work for

you?" He asked as he began helping her remove her trench coat.

"Maybe," she giggled as she stared at her husband's flawless body, encased only in a pair of red boxer briefs.

Once Trent removed his wife's coat, his gaze wandered over her lace-clad body. He appreciated that after six children with his wife, her body still looked exactly the way it did when he met her. Whether it be good genes, working out endlessly or a few nip tucks here and there she kept herself intact.

"You stare any harder or longer my husband will have a bone to pick with you."

Trent glanced down at his boxers, "Forget your husband, I have a bone for you." He whispered. He found it harder and harder to breath in the air around his gorgeous wife.

"You are a trip." Shia shook her head laughing.

Trent took her hand, "Join me in the Jacuzzi."

"Okay, I would love to," she told him.

Stripping down to their birthday suits, they entered the warm water together. Trent sat with his back to the tub and moved Shia to sit in between his legs. He handed her a glass of wine, before picking up his own.

Shia relaxed against her husband's chest and closed her eyes, feeling some of the stress leave her body. She'd needed this.

Putting his glass down, Trent began running Shia's shoulders.

"Mmm, that feels wonderful."

Placing her glass down, Shia shut her eyes and enjoyed the magic her husband's hands were performing on her body.

A few minutes later Shia's soft, even breathing filled the air. Trent looked down at his wife's face, noticing that she had fallen asleep.

Careful not to wake her as he climbed out the Jacuzzi, he lifted her into his arms and grabbed a towel as he exited the bathroom. Placing the towel on the bed, he laid her atop the towel. Returning to the bathroom, he grabbed another towel and went back to the bed to dry her off. Once done, he pulled the comforter back, placed her underneath, and pulled the comforter up to her chin so that she wouldn't get cold.

Grabbing one of the towels, Trent began drying himself off

and then climbed into bed next to his wife pulling her into his embrace. He was perfectly content listening to her breathing beside him for the rest of the night. Kissing her eyebrow, he closed his eyes and joined his wife in slumber.

CHAPTER 18

A light knock at his hotel door jarred him out of his deep slumber.

"Housekeeping." A female voice said from the other side of the door.

Trent glanced down at his watch. It was 6:15 in the morning, what could housekeeping want at this hour. Realizing his bed was empty and his wife was gone, he grabbed the towel he had dried off with the night before and wrapped it around his waist. Walking up to the door and glancing through the peephole, he saw a woman in uniform standing next to a cart of hotel supplies.

"Yes?" He said, opening the door a hint of a question in his voice. When he made eye contact with the woman, his body tensed in recognition. "Phylicia." He whispered.

"The one and only!" She smiled, "Looks like I came at the right time," she said taking in the chiseled body that greeted her in only a towel. Shoving the gun that she had resting on the cart under a stack of towels, "Well, aren't you going to invite your dear old friend in for a visit?"

Noticing the gun, Trent stepped back into the room and allowed her to enter.

"You act like you aren't pleased to see me. How about a little hug for old time's sake?"

"No, I'd rather not." Trent told her as he stood his ground. He wasn't afraid of Phylicia, she had a way of taking everything that mattered to him away in some form or fashion, and at this point, he didn't care anymore. He turned his back on her and sat in the chair at the desk in the room. "What can I do for you this morning?"

Phylicia stared at him, finding this moment unreal. She had been waiting for some alone time with Trent and here it was.

"I've missed you."

"Did you take my daughter?" Trent asked her ignoring her statement.

"Your daughter is missing?" Phylicia asked him innocently. "I had no idea. How many children do you have now?"

Her lackadaisical attitude irritated Trent. "I'm not playing games with you anymore, Phylicia. You've already ruined my life. I don't care anymore. I know you have Luna. You can do what you want with me, but please return her to Shia. If you love me as you say you do, please return her to her mother. Don't harm her in any way."

"I don't know what you're talking about."

Trent snorted. "Sure you don't." He rested his hands behind his head, "So what do you want? You made it a point to seek me out. Okay, you've found me. Now what?" He thoroughly regretted giving this woman his business card years ago in the museum. When all the items fell out of her purse that day, he should have left her right there to pick them up herself. He found it amazing that one moment in time could control your entire life from then on. He couldn't understand, after all these years, why there was not one man in the whole entire world that Phylicia could latch on to and finally be able to let him go.

"I want what I have always wanted...You." Phylicia told him matter of factly.

Trent narrowed his eyes at her, wondering what he used to see and how he didn't know she had a mental illness when he first met her.

"Phylicia you do realize how crazy and bizarre this sounds, right?" He eyed her intently. "It's been decades since we've dated. How can you hold on to me so long? I've lived out a whole life with someone else and I've been happy. Why won't you allow yourself the same luxury? After all this time, I think it is fair to say that you really need to let me go."

Phylicia listened to the words that came out of Trent's mouth and each one felt like a dagger thrown at her heart.

"I love you Trent. I've always loved you. The one incident that separated us wasn't my fault."

Trent could see her softening, "I know it wasn't, but I didn't know that at the time. Just because you finally came clean about it doesn't give you the right to come back and try to take over my life. What we had was good when we had it, but that was long ago. I've found my life mate and I will die by her side. Listen to what I'm saying to you. I will never as long as I have breath in my lungs leave Shia. She is the world to me and I will never let her go."

"How can you say that?" Phylicia shouted, enraged, "She let you go. That's why you're here in this hotel. I never would have left you, even if I were mad at you. I'm loyal. A true ride or die till the end."

Trent closed his eyes momentarily and prayed that the Lord would help him deal with this situation by giving him strength. There needed to be peace in his life. "I know Phylicia, I know. That is one of the things that I loved and love about you; you never made me question your loyalty for a moment until the baby incident." He told her and that was a genuine response.

If the baby incident never occurred, paternity never became an issue, and Phylicia hadn't been married at the time, he would have had a completely different life; and she would be his wife. Their daughter Khloe would still be alive and probably getting ready to graduate high school. However, life hasn't worked out like that. It was time Phylicia came to grips with what was and what was going to be.

"But that incident wasn't my fault." Phylicia whined.

"I know that now and if you had taken the time to explain the situation to me back then or trusted me with what you were going through, we wouldn't be standing here twenty years later trying to fantasize about what could have been. We have to focus on the facts and real life. In this *real* life, I am married to Shia. We have six children that we are raising and if you return my baby, I would be grateful to you."

"Who said that I have your bab--?"

"You have her." Trent interrupted. "Stop playing these games. I know you have her, you know you have her, the only question I have is, are you returning her today or tomorrow?" Trent was done playing games with Phylicia. If she was going to kill him, so be it. Come what may, Luna would be returned to Shia so that his wife could be okay.

Phylicia knew her bonding session with Trent was ending. Clutching the weapon in her hand, she aimed it at him.

Trent didn't flinch or have any reaction when she pointed the weapon at him. "I don't care anymore, Phylicia. He told her as he stood up and began walking towards her. Can't you see that? I've been through so much with you, my life would be better off if I were dead anyway. I don't care."

It surprised Phylicia that Trent felt that way. What would she do in a world without Trent in it? The only thing that would mean is that she would never find the happiness that she sought with him. Setting the gun back down on the cart, Phylicia stared at Trent with hurt and tears in her eyes. She had reduced him to this and she was angry with herself for forcing the man she loved into this lifestyle.

"I love you." Phylicia told him solemnly, "I owe you a daughter since I took Khloe away from you... from us. I'll return your baby tonight. I owe you that much." The tears that had been threatening to spill fell from her tear ducts. "She never really took to me anyway. Very stubborn." Phylicia smiled softly, "In another life, I could see her being mine. She reminds me so much of Khloe. The day I saw her out in the yard by herself, I just had to have her."

Gazing up at Trent as she sniffed, "I never hurt her, just so you know. I was going to raise her and be her mom," she sniffed again as she shook her head, "You know I never had the opportunity to raise either one of my daughters. I wanted to see what it would be like again. I miss hearing the word mom."

Trent remained silent as Phylicia vented. He didn't want to say or do anything that would deter Phylicia from bringing his daughter home.

"I'll go pick her up. I'll be back." Phylicia told him as she abruptly ended her monologue and left the room.

Trent dropped to his knees, "Thank you Lord. Thank you for having my daughter returned to me."

The figure that had followed Phylicia to the hotel had been waiting patiently in their car outside hoping that Phylicia would exit the building soon. Watching as a housekeeper was leaving for the evening, the figure watched as she approached the car that Phylicia had arrived in. Squinting in the darkness, the figure realized that it was Phylicia. Instead of following her, the figure decided to check into the hotel. Whatever had made Phylicia come here was more than likely going to make her come back and when she returned, the figure would be waiting for her.

Phylicia hopped into her Volkswagen coupe and sped away towards home. Making it back just as the sun was rising, a highly upset Elliott greeted her at the door.

"Where have you been?" His rage barely contained.

Phylicia eyed him suspiciously immediately putting her guard up. "What do you mean?"

She asked innocently, "I left you a note."

"Yes, you did. A note that said you would be right back. It's seven in the morning."

"I brought you breakfast." Phylicia grinned as she held up the McDonald's bag.

"You taking me for a joke will not go well for you." Elliott warned. "I need an answer."

Phylicia stared at him a long time in disbelief, trying to give him the benefit of the doubt since it was obvious that he didn't know to whom he was speaking. Answering in an annoyed tone, "I had to clear my head. I was driving around. Is that okay with you?" She asked smartly placing the McDonald's bag on the kitchen table.

"No, not really," he told her before grabbing his keys and leaving her in the house.

Phylicia let him go. She wasn't in the mood to have a debate with him about what she was doing with her time. She figured she would let him take some time to get it together and check his attitude.

"Aleia! Where are you?"

The toddler slowly made her way into the kitchen where Phylicia was. Thumb stuck in her mouth not saying a word. Phylicia picked her up and carried her to the door, grateful that Elliott had dressed her for the day. Strapping her into the car, she headed back toward the highway and the love of her life, Trent.

CHAPTER 19

Elliott was livid with Shayla. He'd followed her down to Atlanta as she drove Aleia to meet up with some guy. He'd watched her go into the Marriott hotel and he followed as she had taken the stairs to the fifth floor with the sleeping toddler. When she banged on room 521, a tall man had quickly opened the door and taken the sleeping toddler out of her hands, allowed her to enter and shut the door behind her.

Once the door was shut, Elliott crept up to it so that he could listen to what was being said on the other side.

"Are you happy now?" Phylicia asked Trent once she

handed Aleia over to him in one piece.

"Yes, very. Thank you for returning Luna, Phylicia. You don't know how much this means to me."

Phylicia nodded her head, "Yes, I do. That's why I brought her back to you. I love you that much. I already cost you a daughter, it's not fair to take another one."

Trent looked at her and smiled. This was the Phylicia he wished outsiders had an opportunity to see, the woman that had a softer caring side and could see outside of her own wants and desires.

"Thank you. Now I can have my life back," he gazed up at Phylicia, "Can I have my life back? My family is tired of being in hiding. They want to live a normal life and I want that for them."

Phylicia gazed at Trent in earnest. She wanted him to live a normal life, but it has to be with her or he could have no life at all.

"I will allow your family as normal life if you promise me one thing."

"Anything." Trent assured her. "Whatever you want, you can have."

"I just want you. What I've always wanted." Phylicia said, blinking back tears. "If you give me you, I promise to leave your family alone. They can come out of hiding. Not that it did y'all any good anyway," she smirked.

"That's it?" Trent asked, "He wanted to be clear on the terms."

"That's it. Give me you and your family is free to be free."

"Done." Trent told her. "I'm yours."

"Really?" Phylicia asked skeptically.

"Really." Trent told her honestly. He was willing to make this sacrifice for his family. They needed peace and he was going to give them that. "Under one condition."

"Ok, what?" Phylicia stated.

"I want to be able to see my kids finish growing up. If nothing else, I want to be able to visit them and go to their activities. Just be there for them as their dad so that they don't miss out on having one around."

"That may be something we can work out. I don't see a problem with that."

"Good. Then I'm all yours... free for the taking. Just let me take this little one home and you and I will be on our way."

Phylicia smiled in gratitude. She was finally going to get what she wanted after all these years of waiting.

"Tell you what, why don't you take your daughter home, explain the situation to Shia and get my address," she handed him the hotel stationary that she had written on, "and I'll see you tomorrow evening sometime. How does that sound?"

"It sounds wonderful. Thank you for that." Trent told her.

"You're welcome." Phylicia told him as she left the room. She wasn't worried about him not showing up because he already knew the consequences if he chose to do something about that ignorance. She wasn't the least bit worried at all.

CHAPTER 20

Her mother had somehow gotten away. Avionne was heated, that woman was going to get what was coming to her and much sooner than later she thought.

It was time her mother knew what had become of her. Hanging her foster mother Krista had been just the thing she needed to begin finding herself. It felt good. It's wasn't that Krista had done anything wrong except love Avionne too much and she didn't know how to respond to such genuine and true emotion. She had done what she thought was best. She knew that Ms. Krista was in heaven loving on some child that truly deserved it because Avionne never felt she was deserving of love.

Walking into the hotel, she told the concierge that she needed to deliver something to her dad but he wasn't answering his phone. She gave them his name and they gladly let her know his room number. She was no dummy; she knew that Trent was the answer. Wherever he was, there her mother would be also.

Opening the door of his hotel room with a sleeping Luna in his arms, Trent was baffled to see a young woman standing there about to knock.

"Hi, long time no see."

Trent stopped when he saw the petite young woman standing in front of him. For a moment he was back at the Museum of Modern Art staring at a girl that had just dropped the entire contents of her purse on the floor."

"Phylicia?" He whispered. Wondering what she was doing back so soon.

"No. Avionne," she snapped, "You don't remember me?"

Trent snapped out of his trance. "Avionne? Avionne as in Phylicia's daughter, Avionne?"

"The one and only in the flesh." She told him.

Now it made sense. Trent thought. No wonder he'd had a flashback. She looked so much like her mother and for one brief moment, he'd been tempted to hug her.

"Wow. How have you been?" Trent asked.

"Not so good."

Trent eyed Avionne warily as he continued to hold Luna in his arms; wondering if she were anything like her mother. He was having a hard time dealing with one psycho in his life. He knew for a fact that there was no way that he would be able to survive two of them.

"I'm sorry to hear that. Is there anything I can do to help?"

"I'm looking for my mother." Avionne told him getting right to business, not interested in small talk.

Trent eyed her in confusion. "Why would you seek me out to ask about *your* mother?"

"Please don't play games with me sir. I don't have time to waste." Avionne told him in all seriousness. "She's obsessed with you. Wherever you are, she is. Please help me."

Trent wondered what Avionne could want after all this time and why Phylicia hadn't sought her out. If her mother had wanted to see her, she would have.

Trent's silence was annoying Avionne. "You're not going to answer me?" She asked him.

"I already know she was here I saw here, but I lost her outside. My mother is the queen of eluding and disappearing." Staring at Trent with bright brown eyes, she tried to work the little girl angle. "Please help me kind sir, I miss my mommy."

Trent was no fool. He had seen all of this before. Avionne was an exact replica of Phylicia at that age and he knew that meant she was up to no good. He had no time for her or her games.

"If you were smart enough to find your mother and follow her here one time, then you are smart enough to know she will probably return."

"Please don't speak to me like that. I know how intelligent I am and I realize she may be coming back here, but I don't want to wait around that long to see her. Do you understand?" She pointedly asked Trent, not in the mood for his adolescent mind games. The nerve of him questioning her intelligence, yet he was the one in protective custody out of fear of her mother. Shaking her head, she was offended.

"I don't know where your mother is and even if I did know, she obviously doesn't want to see you. Otherwise, she would have come for you by now. Did you ever think of that?"

"Now, now," Avionne began as she pulled a gun out of her purse, "Watch your mouth when you speak to me. You never know what my *smart* self may have up my sleeve. You were once like a dad to me; don't go scraping at wounds that have never healed. That can get you into a heap of trouble. Mind your manners, please."

Trent shook his head, "Like mother, like daughter," he said. For the first time in his life, he was grateful that Khloe was no longer here. He would have hated for her to turn out anything like her mother Phylicia or older sister, Avionne. Raising his eyes to the ceiling, he sent up a silent prayer. Seems as if the Lord always knows what's best and just this one time he was very thankful.

"I am nothing like her!" Avionne shouted, getting directly in front of Trent's face. "I'm a better woman than she ever will be."

Trent shrugged, "If you say so." Not phased in the least by Avionne. He dealt with her lion of a mother for a living. In comparison, she was a field mouse.

Avionne wanted to beat that indifferent attitude out of Trent but knew that if she hurt a hair on his head, she would become a target for her mother. She wasn't in a position at the moment to have those types of issues.

"You're not going to tell me where my mother is? Even with a gun pointed at you?"

"No." Trent shook his head, "If you were going to use it, you would have done it by now. I have never done anything to you, but treat you as my own when you were younger. With all that to consider, why would you pull the trigger now?"

Avionne considered what he was saying. Maybe *he* was smarter than *she* thought.

"If anything," Trent continued, "I think that you need a hug," he softened his tone. "Would you like me to give you one?"

Avionne stared into Trent's welcoming face and her composure slipped. "I would love a hug." She surprised herself by saying those words as she set the weapon down. Trent walked over to lay Luna on the sofa Luna before coming back to embrace her. Avionne allowed herself to welcome the first genuine hug she could remember experiencing.

Avionne pulled at Trent's heartstrings. He remembered her being a little girl and now here she was in the flesh. He felt bad when he realized he should have checked on her throughout the years to make sure that she was good, but he hadn't done that. He was just as guilty of neglecting her as her own mother was.

"Why don't you get a room here tonight? Your mother will be back at some point and at the very least, you will be close.

My treat." Trent told Avionne as she stepped out of the embrace.

Trent knew that Phylicia wasn't coming back to the hotel because he was checking out today.

Avionne smiled up at Trent. "That would be wonderful. Thank you so much," she was sure she had more money than he did, but there was no reason to let him know that. However, he was a great guy; she could see why her mother was infatuated.

CHAPTER 21

Elliott was seeing red as he stood waiting for Shayla when she exited the Marriott. "This is what you have been doing with your time? Who was that man?" he busted out as soon as he saw her.

Phylicia narrowed her eyes, surprised to see Elliott standing by her car in the parking lot. "You followed me?"

"You bet your life I followed you," he said harshly, "You've been all secretive. Did you think I wouldn't be curious as to where my woman was heading all hours of the night?"

Phylicia was sad for Elliott. She couldn't care less about what he was speaking of as she said a mini prayer for his soul in her head.

"Why did you leave your daughter with that man?"

Phylicia shrugged, "That's none of your business," she said as she attempted to push past him so that she could gain access to her car.

Elliott pushed her back catching her off guard, causing her to fall backward onto the pavement.

Phylicia was shell-shocked as she sat on the ground, staring up at Elliott, observing him in a new light.

"You think I don't know who you are, Shayla? Better yet Phylicia?" Elliott gave her a pointed look, "I make it my business to know everyone that I deal with."

Phylicia began clapping very disrespectfully from her sitting position. She was angry with herself for allowing this to be able to happen. She was slippin' and clearly losing her touch. The old Phylicia never would have allowed anyone to catch her off guard like this, she thought. It was definitely time to hang it up.

Any good thing ending needed a last hurrah and a last hurrah she was going to have.

"So you do a little research and you think you've got me all figured out now? Is that what it is?" Phylicia asked him incredulously as she pushed herself up to a standing position not wanting to bring any unwanted attention their way.

"Don't I?" Elliott asked.

Phylicia shrugged, "You tell me. You're the one over here spitting knowledge... maybe I'll learn something as you continue talking." She told him sarcastically.

Elliott raised his hand and slapped Phylicia across her face. No one spoke to him in such a manner and got away with it. She wasn't going to be the first.

Phylicia touched her tongue to her lip, tasting the blood where she felt a small cut from where Elliott had hit her. Her temper wanted to flare up, but she didn't allow it. He wanted to feel as if he was in a power position and she wanted that for him.

"Do you feel better now?" She asked him. "Can we please go back to the house and not fight in a parking lot?"

Elliott eyed her skeptically. He'd done his research. He wasn't afraid of her, but he also knew that she couldn't be trusted.

"We can finish this discussion at home if that will make you more comfortable."

"Thank you. I don't want to cause a scene here and would feel more comfortable at home."

Phylicia took her key lock out of her pocket and unlocked her car as Elliott opened the door for her to get in. As soon as she was inside and he closed her car door, she sped off without giving her car a moment's time to warm up.

****

Arriving at the house considerably sooner than Elliott, Phylicia quickly began taking the bulbs out of each light fixture in the house, as well as making sure every door and window in the house was locked. Acting fast, she went to the hall closet and plugged each iron she owned into a wall socket giving them time to heat up. Pulling her long hair into a ponytail, she moved every knife she owned in the kitchen out the cabinet drawer and dropped them into the laundry basket in the basement. All pots and pans were placed inside the washing machine. Phylicia was on her way to grab some rope when she heard Elliott's truck pull into the driveway.

Walking slowly to a window at the side of the house, she watched as he exited his truck at a snail's pace and moved his head from side to side seeming to try to take in his surroundings. Phylicia smirked as he made his way to the front door. What an amateur. She thought as she waited for the front door to open. After a few minutes with no motion, her head snapped toward the den when she heard what sounded like a window resisting a push. Remaining in her location Phylicia stayed crouched in the shadows. She never went towards danger, danger had to come to her, and from there they would duke it out. Breathing in and out slowly as to not make much noise she forced her hearing sense to pick up. Turning her head to the right, she heard a noise in the bathroom; she listened as the glass broke.

Phylicia knew better though. The glass breaking was a decoy. Elliott had no intention of coming in through the miniature bathroom window. His plan was to get her to go in there to trap her, but Phylicia knew better. She laughed silently to herself; he was dealing with a professional. His body count probably hasn't even hit ten yet. She thought to herself and he thought he was ready to take her on. She was excited, as it had been a long time since she was in a game of cat & mouse and she had the patience to play all night.

After a full ten minutes went by with no action or sound, Phylicia smiled when she heard faint footsteps on the stairs coming from the basement. "Bout time." She thought. Let the games begin! The door to the basement creaked open and then stopped. If Phylicia weren't playing this game of life with him, she would have laughed. "Oh Elliott," she thought. Unhooking a knife from her ankle clip and threw it across the room.

"Ahhhh." Elliott yelled out. Glancing down, he realized that a knife had struck him in his left side. Clutching his side, he pulled the knife out fast before it did more damage. Blood continued to ooze out of the spot.

Phylicia smiled when she hit her target. Assassins 101 know how to be a knife thrower, she thought. He was pathetic. What did I ever see in him? She thought to herself.

"You Bitch!" Elliott screamed in pain as he staggered around by the stairs.

Saying nothing, Phylicia pulled another knife from her ankle clip. Aiming at his neck this time, she flicked her wrist and let the knife sail through the air.

"Ahhhhhhhhhhhhhhhhhhhhhh." Elliott yelled as he tried to grab his neck, but losing his balance in the process and falling back down the basement stairs.

Phylicia ran to the steps as swift as a ninja. Gazing down the staircase to see Elliott withering in pain, she shook her head, "First guy I date in over a decade and I choose a wimp." Pulling another knife out of her ankle clip, she watched him for a minute before aiming the knife directly at his face. She was pleased when his withering stopped and was now reduced to only moaning. Walking down the stairs as graceful as a swan, Phylicia stood over Elliott, who had a gash oozing blood in his side, a knife stuck in his chest and the last knife Phylicia had thrown protruding out of one of his eye sockets, he was a sight for sore eyes.

Standing over top of him as he continued to moan, Phylicia straddled him and knelt down so that she could sit on his chest, which meant also sitting on the knife that with the extra force went directly through his heart.

Jerking as the knife went through his body, Elliott's one good eye tried to focus on Phylicia's face illuminated only by the glimpses of light through the blinds from the streetlights. "Why?"

"Because you did not know your place. Look at you now as you struggle to breathe." She crossed her arms and leaned down staring into his one good eye. "You started a war you weren't equipped to win." Phylicia watched as his breathing became more and more ragged before she felt his heart pump no more. Eyeing one of the irons that she had plugged in she retrieved it and brought it over to Elliott. Even though he was dead, she couldn't resist holding the hot iron to his skin and smiling as his flesh began to burn.

I'm hungry, Phylicia realized as she stood up unplugging the iron and bouncing up the basement stairs, leaving Elliott to rot in his own blood. Tacos are just what the doctor ordered she thought as she entered the kitchen to begin thawing out ground beef on the stove in preparation for her dinner.

CHAPTER 22

S hia answered her cell groggily. She stayed in Trent's hotel room late again the previous night and her body was reminding her quite effectively that she wasn't the young spring chicken that she used to be and that these late night on the creep sex sessions she was having with her husband was not helping. They had decided that Trent would spend a few more nights at the hotel so that they could try to put the spice back into their relationship. The sex was good, the not getting much sleep was the part she was having a rough time with and was not the business.

"Good Morning," she whispered into the phone.

"Mmm, sounds like a good night from over here." A low deep voice laughed.

"Baby." Shia half cried, half groaned. "Why are you calling me so early?"

Trent smirked into the phone, "You're going to regret that statement once you hear what I have to say and you will be very grateful about what I have to say to you."

"I'll be the judge of that." Shia croaked as she lay with her eyes closed waiting to hear what he had to say."

"You're *so* gonna owe me." Trent said continuing to play.

"Oh my God Trent, what do you want? Did you just call to wake me up to play on my phone?" Shia laughed tiredly.

"Okay, okay, okay your highness. No, I did not just call to wake you up or play on your phone, but either way I wanted to hear your voice."

Shia remained quiet waiting for her husband to get to the point refusing to entertain him any longer.

Trent got the hint through her silence, "I have a little present for you."

"You are my present. What can be greater than you?" Shia commented.

Trent smiled, "You're my gift every day of my life to babe, but this present is amazing. This is the second time that I get to announce to you this package has ten fingers and ten toes and we will call her Luna. She's a little heavier this go round though."

Shia's eyes sprang open and she quickly sat up on the bed. "What? What do you mean?"

"I mean, right here in my arms is a little bundle of joy that calls me daddy and what do you call her?" He asked someone in the background.

"Mommy!" A chipper voice came across Shia's airwaves.

"Luna! My baby, oh my gosh! Are you okay?"

"Yes, Mommy. Daddy got me some ice cream."

Shia tried to laugh, but was too choked up with emotion, "Did he? Is it good?"

"Yes. I miss you Mommy."

Shia closed her eyes and held the phone so close to her face that they may as well have been fused together. "I miss you to punkin. I love you."

"Love you too Mommy."

"I have her babe, she's safe. We're on the way to the house now." Trent said into the receiver reclaiming control of his cell.

"This is crazy! I am so glad you called me this morning. I apologize for giving you such a hard time."

"I didn't take it personally. I'm used to you." Trent laughed, "We'll be there in about five minutes. So up and at 'em."

"You're so silly. Okay, see you two in a few." Shia said, hanging up the phone.

****

As the door opened, Shia was in a state of shock. She couldn't believe what was happening. Tears began streaming down her face so hard she had to keep blinking fixing her blurry vision. There in her doorway was her estranged husband holding a baby girl, her baby girl Luna had finally made her way home.

"Mommy!"

"Oh my God." Shia exclaimed as Luna leapt into her arms. "My baby has returned home. Thank you, God. Thank you, God," she said wiping her eyes as she held the toddler tightly refusing to let Luna go. "Prayer changes everything. I knew in my heart that my baby would come back to us. I knew it."

Luna's eyes were closed as she held onto her mother. Tears also escaped the little girls face. Shia was beside herself. Her baby being kidnapped had consumed her. Now she just wanted to hold her and never let her go again. She was still finding it hard to believe that she was home again. Her baby girl was here in her arms, it all seemed so surreal to her.

"Hey baby, how was your day?" Trent asked entering their house waving at Shia trying to get her attention. "Doesn't the delivery boy get a kiss, or do they all go to the found princess?" "I'm so sorry!" Shia said leaning up to kiss Trent as he bent down to her, she hadn't meant to be dismissive of him. She was just bursting with excitement.

"Luna is like right here!" She exclaimed.

Trent chuckled, "I know, I brought her to you."

"I need to talk to you for a minute. Let you sisters take Luna for a second."

Shia stopped smiling once she detected the seriousness in Trent's tone. "What's wrong?" She asked suddenly worried as she allowed Remi to remove Luna out of her grasp.

Trent took her hand and led her into the den. "Have a seat."

Shia sat in the chair closest to her wondering what in the world had Trent so uptight.

Rubbing his hands, down his head and face, he looked at her with misery in his gaze, "I did something that you are going to be very upset about."

Shia narrowed her eyes, not uttering a word waiting for him to continue. Whatever it was, she knew that it couldn't possibly be that bad.

"I saw Phylicia."

Shia's blood immediately began to boil, but she was trying to give Trent the benefit of the doubt and listen.

"That's how we got Luna back. You were right. She had her the entire time."

Shia shook her head, not understanding how Trent could still be this stupid when it came to that woman. "We have Luna back. I don't care how you did it. My daughter is home. Whatever it is, I will forgive you."

"I have to go live with Phylicia." Trent sighed.

"WHAT! Are you crazy? You're not going to live with her. You better think again. I'm not having it." Shia jumped out of her chair. "Why the hell did you come in here with that nonsense thinking it was going to fly with me?" She eyeballed Trent incredulously.

"I don't have a choice. Either I go along with her program or she continues to prey on my family. At least this way, you all can live in peace and I'll know you're safe." Trent dropped his head, "I have to keep my family safe baby. I have to."

Shia knew he was going through an internal struggle, but that didn't make things any easier on her end. She was beside herself and not happy at all.

"Why can't we just report her, and be done with this? You know how to get in contact with her now. Let's end it."

Trent shook his head, "For what purpose, so she can break out again and track us down again? Our whole life has been an ongoing déjà vu record that I want to end."

"And you think that by giving her what she wants, meaning you, it will somehow calm down her psychotic ways? Nothing can tame her, Trent. She is a lost cause and you keep hoping against hope that it will be different. Why?" Shia stared at him, but she knew, "Because you still love her, huh?" Shaking her head, she gazed at him in disappointment. "I should have known. After all these years, you still carry a flame. How pathetic," she looked at him in disgust. "Do what you have to do. I'm done with this. I'm going to spend time with my baby."

Not knowing what else there was to say, Trent gathered his belongings and left the house headed to the address Phylicia had provided him.

****

She had chosen to follow Trent when he left the hotel knowing he had been much too eager for her to get a room for that night. Something told Avionne that he wouldn't be returning and it turns out that she was right. Turns out, she was just that intelligent after all. She thought smugly.

Avionne watched the family reunion from a distance. With her binoculars, she was able to see inside the home that Trent shared with his family. She keyed in on his perfect little family, how pathetic she thought. No wonder her mother trailed behind Trent, she craved for what he had between his wife and children.

Avionne could understand that. Not too long ago, she wanted some kind of family tie, but not anymore. Love was for the weak spirited and she was anything but that. Once upon a time, Avionne had honestly wanted to get to know her mother. Since life hadn't afforded her the opportunity to get to know her, she was over it. At twenty, she was a grown woman and no longer believed in fairy tales or the lies they told.

Watching Trent as he left the house with a bag slung over his arm, she started her car and followed him as he drove toward the highway. Glad that she had a full tank of gas, Avionne made sure to trail Trent at a decent distance so he wouldn't know someone was following him. Avionne turned her music up and jammed out with Gwen Stefani the entire ride.

Trent was in his feelings about a multitude of things at the moment. He knew that Shia was writing him off. They were already having a tough time with one another and this change in events wasn't helping any. He did not intend to stay with Phylicia; he was just trying to do what was necessary to keep his family safe for the foreseeable future. Buying them all time until he could find a suitable solution that would work for everyone.

Five hours later, after being lost in his thoughts, Trent turned into a cul de sac, whereas Avionne kept straight, then looped around the neighborhood and came back; just in time to see her mother look towards her car and close the door.

CHAPTER 23

There was a nagging feeling buried at the core of her body. The universe wasn't lining up the way it was supposed to and the feeling forced Phylicia to stay on edge.

"What's wrong with you?" Trent asked as he gazed up at Phylicia who had stood up suddenly from lying on the bed.

"I don't know. Something isn't right," she told him.

Trent had only been there for fifteen minutes and Phylicia had every intention on seducing him, but something was causing her to be uneasy. Standing clad in a red lace teddy with the nipples cut out and a matching red lace mask on, she was ready, however the mood was quickly slipping away from her.

Trent sat up on the bed glancing around the room not seeing anything out of the ordinary. Phylicia had the lights off and candles lit. The only thing he could see were their shadows bouncing off the walls. He personally didn't care one way or the other and was happy about the distraction. He was missing Shia and would give anything to be home with her and their children right now.

"I bet when you had no idea that I would be coming for you today." A low voice whispered from the shadows.

Trent jumped off the bed in surprise at the voice and cut on the light switch.

Phylicia remained unmoved. She held her head up and stared straight into reflective brown eyes, the ones of her daughter.

"I knew you would come." Phylicia told her softly, "You needed to see me for yourself. I've been waiting for you."

Avionne flinched at her words, "You did not know."

Phylicia smiled, "Of course I knew. You only found me because I wanted you to find me. How else would I receive the opportunity to talk to my baby? You're my flesh and blood. I birthed you. Anything you feel, I feel. I know you better than you think I do. Probably better than you know yourself."

That statement angered Avionne. "I am not your baby! You don't know a thing about me!" Avionne snaked her neck to the side. "Only a mother that raised her daughter would know her child and you are no mother of mine." Avionne spat at her.

"That's where you're wrong. I may not have raised you, but I am most definitely your mother. It is my blood that flows through your veins whether you like it or not and don't you forget it!" Phylicia focused narrow eyes on her. "You turned out just like me anyway," she said saddened by the reality of what was.

It was taking everything in Avionne not to tear up. This was a poignant moment for her. Her biological mother was standing right in front of her in arms reach and she didn't know if she wanted to hug her or choke her. She couldn't remember her mother's touch and with her so close, she almost let down her guard. Almost.

Phylicia could see the inner struggle in Avionne and she hurt for her. Her daughter was young and still able to feel things. Phylicia commended her for that because around Avionne's age was a pivotal turning point in Phylicia's own life. She went over the deep end and she knew she was wanted by the world and hated by many. The little bit of good left in her didn't want Avionne to turn out as she did. Her baby still had a chance.

"I will never be able to forget that as long as I breathe air in my lungs, I will know that I am your daughter; which means, I will never know peace as long as I live on this earth."

Tears welled in Phylicia's eyes. "Avionne, what is it that you want from me?"

"Nothing. There is nothing you can do for me, mother." She spoke sarcastically, "Birthing me was enough. I guess I should thank you for that, huh? Thank you," she spat.

Phylicia stared at the beautiful, angry creature in front of her and became remorseful that she was the reason that Avionne was this way. This is what she had been reduced to... looking at her, Phylicia felt a pang of regret. If she hadn't been chasing behind Trent for years she may have gotten an opportunity to see her daughter grow up and excel in life. She had the brains to do it, but there is too much me in her. Phylicia thought as she refused to give her child the benefit of a response.

"Answer me!" Avionne shouted. "I'm dying over here. I want to hug my mother so bad. I love you, but I hate you too. How could you leave me and never come looking for me? Never check on me? Never wonder if I'm okay? I was left alone in the world. I had no one."

The tears Phylicia had been trying to avoid falling could no longer be contained. "I love you too." She told her baby girl. "I love you so much. I did check on you. I have visited you on your birthday every year since the year I escaped that hospital. Every single year. I have always been in your corner looking out for you. I didn't miss not one birthday. Not one." Phylicia reiterated.

"I saw you graduate high school, early I might add. Very proud mama standing over here. I saw you graduate college with honors." Phylicia smiled through her tears. "I didn't miss anything. I remember the long pastel yellow fitted gown you wore to prom with a flower in your hair. My little senorita I called you. You were gorgeous that night."

Avionne gasped in disbelief, "You were there," she whispered.

"I told you I never missed a moment. If nothing else, I did see my baby grow up. I may have watched from a distance, but I was there."

"That doesn't matter now." Avionne was upset with herself for showing any vulnerability around this woman. "You're the reason my life was as hard as it was."

"How hard was your life really, Avionne? Let's talk about it." Phylicia told her, "Whatever is on your chest just let it out so maybe you can deal with this and move on."

"So who are you Iyanla now? You think that you can fix my life. Well, you can't! My life is broken and it is your fault. You did this to me."

"Avionne, you're an adult. If something is wrong with your life, fix it. You can't blame me forever."

"This is so comical coming from Phylicia Lynn Taylor. The same woman who spent her whole adult life chasing after a man that never wanted her in the first place."

Avionne's last statement had Phylicia seeing red. "You don't know what you're talking about so I think it's best for you to be quiet now or did you not get the memo of what happened to your sister." Phylicia smiled smugly at her.

Avionne laughed, "So you're threatening me now? How typical of you." Shaking her head in disgust, Avionne pulled the gun from behind her back. "You don't know what it takes to be a mother. And I've had enough of you."

Trent stared in horror at the two women, secretly wanting Avionne to pull the trigger so that he could go home and his family could live in peace.

Avionne stared Phylicia square in the eye and an unflinching Phylicia stared back at her. She'd known that it would come to this. Avionne had too much rage in her. Phylicia could stop her if she wanted to, but this was one fight she wanted and deserved to lose.

"Good-bye Avi," Phylicia whispered as a single tear slid down her cheek. "I love you. This is the way things should be."

"Good-bye, mother." Avi said, unmoved by her mother's tear.

BANG!

Email Mychea at: mychea@mychea.com

www.mychea.com

Books by Good2Go Authors on Our Bookshelf

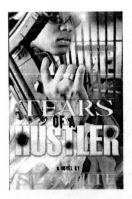

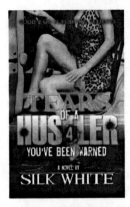

Good2Go Films Presents

To order books, please fill out the order form below:

To order films please go to www.good2gofilms.com

Name: _____

Address: _____

City: _____ State: _____ Zip Code: _____

Phone: _____

Email: _____

Method of Payment: ☐ Check ☐ VISA ☐ MASTERCARD

Credit Card#: _____

Name as it appears on card: _____

Signature: _____

Item Name	Price	Qty	Amount
48 Hours to Die – Silk White	$14.99		
He Loves Me, He Loves You Not - Mychea	$14.99		
He Loves Me, He Loves You Not 2 - Mychea	$14.99		
He Loves Me, He Loves You Not 3 - Mychea	$14.99		
Married To Da Streets – Silk White	$14.99		
My Boyfriend's Wife - Mychea	$14.99		
Never Be The Same – Silk White	$14.99		
Stranded – Silk White	$14.99		
Slumped – Jason Brent	$14.99		
Tears of a Hustler - Silk White	$14.99		
Tears of a Hustler 2 - Silk White	$14.99		
Tears of a Hustler 3 - Silk White	$14.99		
Tears of a Hustler 4- Silk White	$14.99		
Tears of a Hustler 5 – Silk White	$14.99		
Tears of a Hustler 6 – Silk White	$14.99		
The Panty Ripper - Reality Way	$14.99		
The Teflon Queen – Silk White	$14.99		
The Teflon Queen 2 – Silk White	$14.99		
The Teflon Queen – 3 – Silk White	$14.99		
The Teflon Queen 4 – Silk White	$14.99		
Time Is Money - Silk White	$14.99		
Young Goonz – Reality Way	$14.99		
Subtotal:			
Tax:			
Shipping (Free) U.S. Media Mail:			
Total:			

Make Checks Payable To: Good2Go Publishing
7311 W Glass Lane, Laveen, AZ 85339

CPSIA information can be obtained at www.ICGtesting.com
Printed in the USA
LVOW07s1706090116

469908LV00017B/919/P